VOID WRAITH

VOID WRAITH BOOK 2

CHRIS FOX

CHRIS FOX WRITES, LLC

For Pat and Kathy, two of the most amazing people I know.

PREVIOUSLY ON VOID WRAITH

Whenever I pick up the 2nd book in a series I'm always torn. Should I re-read the first book, or just dive right in? I usually want to do the latter, but I can't always remember what happened in the previous book. This section is for all those people who can't quite remember everything that went down in *Destroyer*. I've decided to re-cap it just like a TV show, something fans of my *Deathless* series have really enjoyed. For those that have just finished *Destroyer*, feel free to skip to the Prologue.

Also note that I'm not including information about the prequel story *Exiled* here. If you haven't read it, I recommend it. It will introduce you to Delta, Reid, Kathryn, Annie, and Bock, plus you'll learn how Nolan was exiled to the 14th fleet. You can get it for free by signing up to the mailing list.

In an announcer voice: 'Last time, on Void Wraith..."

Commander Nolan has just been assigned to the *UFC Johnston*, an aging destroyer in the 14th fleet. The 14th is also known as "the underfunded 14th," where careers are sent to die. The *Johnston* is commanded by Captain Dryker, an aging hero from the Eight-Year War with the Tigris. He's tired, cantankerous, and has a serious discipline problem.

The *Johnston* is emerging from a sun, through something called a Helios Gate. The Helios Gate is at the center of a star, and opens a wormhole to a neighboring star. Starships that want to use the Helios Gate have to be able to survive the internal stresses inside a star, which they do using their inductive fields. This field channels the magnetic energy inside a star to form a bubble around the ship. The sun itself powers the field, so the deeper a vessel goes the stronger the field gets.

Make sense? If not, think of it like this: it's a frigging Stargate in the middle of a sun.

The *Johnston* has arrived in the Mar Kona system, a human colony on the periphery of space. They've been dispatched because the colony has gone dark and OFI (the Office of Fleet Intelligence, known by the soldiers of the 14th as the Office of F*%cking Idiots) is demanding answers. Upon arrival, they find a debris field belonging to a Tigris science vessel.

There's no reason for a Tigris science vessel to be there, and no sign of whoever or whatever destroyed it. Then a Tigris warship arrives, looking for the science vessel. They assume the *Johnston* is responsible for the destruction, and move to attack. Captain Dryker does something no real captain would do. Ever. He walks off the bridge in combat, leaving the untested Commander Nolan to run the combat. Fiction lets me get away with crap like this.

Unsurprisingly, Nolan pulls off a brilliant maneuver that Michael Bay will enjoy producing because there are plenty of *pew pew BOOOOM* sorts of things involved. The Tigris lose, and Captain Dryker sends Nolan down to the planet with a squad of Marines to find out why the citizens are gone. If you've played Mass Effect, by this point you were probably asking yourself how long it would be before EA sued me, because MAN did the plot of *Destroyer* look similar.

Nolan and company run into a new enemy. This enemy has an imperfect cloaking system, a lot like the one used in Halo and Predator. The enemy clashes with the Marines, and there are casualties on both sides. Unfortunately, the enemies explode when they die, so it's difficult for Nolan to learn specifics about who or what they might be. They look like robots, but when Mills (handsome badass sniper dude) cores one through the chest they see orange blood spatter the trees.

Nolan and his Marines continue toward the distress signal they picked up in orbit. They find it in the middle of a set of ancient Primo ruins. Primo are the first race (primo means first in Latin), and have been on the galactic stage for tens of thousands of years. Their empire has waned, and as it faded they abandoned many habitable worlds, which races like humanity are all too happy to snap up.

Anyway, it turns out the distress signal was set by Lena, a Tigris scientist. Tigris are a race of bipedal cat people. Why cat people when they've been used everywhere from Thundercats to the Kilrathi? Because I have two house cats named Izzy and Fizgig, and I was looking for an excuse to write about them.

Lena is investigating the Primo ruins, because after laying dormant for over twenty millennia they are starting to power up. She tells Nolan that while she was investigating, her team was attacked. A strange blue ship showed up, and took her team as well as all the citizens of Mar Kona.

She has no idea why, and was only able to hide because the Primo ruins blocked the enemy scans.

Nolan realizes Lena is important, and starts escorting her back to his shuttle. On the way, they see the strange blue ship, which can apparently cloak just like the shock troops (later called Judicators). The ship blows up the Primo ruins, and Nolan narrowly escapes.

We flip to Dryker, who gives a report to his superior, Admiral Mendez. Mendez is upset at Dryker for walking off the bridge during combat, but that turns out to be a smoke-screen. He's really calling because Dryker is being hung out to dry. The Tigris claim Dryker blew up their science vessel, and humanity is turning him over for prosecution. The case will be tried by the Primo. Before the call ends, Mendez also asks if Dryker recovered any artifacts from the ruins (*dun dun dun*). We realize immediately that he's a little too interested. Plus, the guy has a thick black beard and smokes a cigar. We already know he's the villain.

Dryker decides not to turn himself over, and has Nolan interrogate their Tigris prisoner. Lena was on Mar Kona because she's an anthropologist specializing in Primo ruins. Several other worlds have been attacked by these mysterious aliens, and she wants to know why. She agrees to help Dryker find answers, and suggests they start on a Tigris world containing a similar set of ruins to those on Mar Kona.

Right after they arrive at Purito, a Tigris warship exits the Helios Gate. This is no privateer, but rather the most feared commander in Leonis Pride, Mighty Fizgig. Fizgig is based on my 16-year-old house cat, who is too old to care about your bullshit. She (the commander, not my cat) contacts Dryker, warning him that she's going to board his vessel and slaughter his crew. Dryker does his best to fight back, but her ship is both larger and more powerful. He's clearly losing.

Meanwhile, Nolan and Lena are trying to find whatever artifact might be hidden in the ruins. While they're exploring, the Tigris send a ground team to stop them. That team is opposed by Sergeant Hannan and her Marines. They square off, locked in a brutal fight. Hannan knows she can't hold the Tigris off forever, but is determined to go down swinging.

Then Fizgig receives a message that a nearby Tigris colony is under attack. She pulls back, letting the *Johnston* go. Fizgig arrives just in time to see the strange alien vessel cloaking. She's now aware there is a new player in the game, but is honor bound to hunt down and kill Dryker rather than investigate.

Lena and Nolan recover an ancient Virtual Intelligence (VI) from the ruins, but can't understand the dialect it uses. Lena is only able to translate two words: Void Wraith. They take the VI to a Primo library, hoping the scholars there can translate it. The Primo do, reluctantly giving the VI back to Lena and Nolan. Because they're spiteful bastards and know the *Johnston* is being hunted, they alert Primo authorities. Dryker orders Nolan back to the *Johnston*, and they get ready to flee.

They're too late. Three Primo carriers show up. The *Johnston* has no prayer, but quickly realize they aren't the target. The carriers attack the library, though the *Johnston* takes some serious collateral damage while escaping. There's some *pew pew pew, boom*, and then the *Johnston* flees to the Helios Gate. The library is blown up, and Nolan and Dryker realize why: someone was trying to keep the ancient Primo VI from spreading. The library made a copy, and someone didn't want that copy getting out.

Meanwhile, we learn that Admiral Mendez is a villain. It's terribly shocking. I mean, he has a beard and cigar, remember? We totally didn't see this coming. His villainy-ness is discovered by his daughter, Kathryn Mendez. Apparently Kathryn is the reason why Nolan got sent to the 14th, but we don't know why because the asshole author wants you to read *Exiled* to find out.

Kathryn learns that her father is working with someone he calls Bruce (Doctor Reid), and that both are clearly working for a third party. It's also revealed that the Primo and Tigris governments have been infiltrated as well. They're working on something big, and it sounds like it will be bad for everyone. Kathryn lets Nolan know, and he brings the information to Dryker. Kathryn overheard something about the Ghantan system, which doesn't show up on any known star chart. Dryker doesn't seem surprised, because he's old and wise and stuff. He also has a beard, but his beard is white so we know he's not a villain.

Lena realizes the Primo VI they recovered might recognize the system. Now that it's been translated, they can talk to it, and she learns that it knows all about the strange blue ship. The ship belongs to the Void Wraith, who wiped out the ancient Primo empire. The Primo VI is very familiar with the Ghantan system, and explains that it was a mining facility, and also contained a Primo shipyard.

The *Johnston* is still heavily damaged, but limps to the Ghantan system to see what's there. It turns out there's a factory building Void Wraith ships, and a big ass bomb. Uh-oh. Nolan and Dryker discuss a plan, and Nolan suggests they go flash their asses to the Goram law (go watch Firefly if you don't get that reference). The *Johnston* uses the Quantum Network to alert the humans, then flies to the Tigris home world.

Dryker talks mad shit over an open channel, and the Tigris start to pursue. That's exactly what he wants, as the goal is to get the whole Tigris fleet to the Ghantan system. It seems to be working, but then the Tigris admiral tells his ships not to pursue. He sends one vessel, Fizgig's *Claw of Tigrana*. Most of the Tigris think this decision strange, but no one does anything.

Fizgig follows Dryker to the Ghantan system and boards his vessel. Dryker surrenders unconditionally, and when Fizgig reaches the bridge, points out the big ass Void Wraith factory and bomb floating like *right there*. Fizgig is all, umm...that looks bad. We should do something about that. Before they can, the Void Wraith attack, and begin boarding the *Johnston*.

Packs of Judicators roam the corridors of the ship, brawling with Marines. All of our heroes step up, and manage to converge on the bridge. They realize they can't win. There are six Void Wraith ships in the system, and just the single ship that's boarded the *Johnston* is handily kicking their collective asses. So Dryker comes up with a daring Hail Mary plan, because he has a white beard. He knows the hero's plan always works at the end, or readers get pissed off and send you hate mail.

He orders Nolan, Fizgig, Izzy (my other house cat), Hannan, and Edwards to EVA (that's Extravehicular activity —going outside the ship) over to the Void Wraith vessel, a harvester-class ship whose troops have boarded the *Johnston*. They're basically doing an end run to take over the enemy ship, since all the enemy's troops are on the *Johnston*. Those who stay behind will hold off the Void Wraith, though they will likely die in the attempt.

Nolan and company head to the Void Wraith vessel. They kick a lot of Judicator ass, including a twelve-foot-tall

Alpha Judicator. Unfortunately, that Judicator squishes Edwards. We're not sure if he'll live yet. The author hasn't killed anyone up to this point. Is he a dick? We don't know.

Back on the *Johnston*, Captain Dryker grabs Mills, Juliard (a comm tech), and the Tigris first mate, Khar. They fight their way toward the *Johnston*'s main gun. Dryker wants to sabotage it, so he can detonate the ship. That will kill all the Judicators aboard, improving Nolan's chances. Along the way they get into a simple skirmish, but during the fight, the causeway Mills is standing on gets hit.

He falls to his death in the most unheroic way possible, despite the fact that he was a total badass. Yup, the author *is* a dick. I still get hate mail about Mills's death, but there was a method to my madness. I needed to show you people that I was serious. Not, like, "George R.R. Martin, kill half the cast" serious, but that anyone could die.

Back to Nolan. He reaches the bridge, which has a VI very similar to the one they liberated from the Primo ruins. The VI monologues like a Disney villain, talking about the Eradication and how Nolan has no prayer. Judicators show up trying to kill them, but Nolan and Hannan hold them off while Lena removes the ship's VI and plugs in the one they got from the ruins. The new VI takes over and merges with the ship, giving them full control.

Around this time, Dryker and Khar set the self destruct and flee for the *Claw of Tigrana*. They make it aboard, but the acting captain is a real douche. He wants to lock up Dryker, instead of listening to him. So Khar snaps his neck and takes over.

A new fleet emerges from the Helios Gate. It's the Tigris! They've come to help Fizgig. Khar tells them about the Void Wraith, and they join the fight. It's an all-out brawl, and it's not clear who's going to win. Then a human fleet arrives!

Except it's under Mendez's control, and is here to help the Void Wraith. It starts attacking Tigris vessels. Khar passes out from blood loss, and Dryker takes command of the Tigris vessel.

A Void Wraith vessel de-cloaks right next to the *Claw*. It's Nolan! He explains that they've figured out where the bomb is being sent. The Void Wraith want to blow up Theras Prime, decapitating the Primo empire. He asks Dryker to flee there and warn the Primo. Dryker reluctantly agrees. He pilots the *Claw* into the sun.

Nolan and his crew come up with a desperate plan to stop the bomb. If they can open a connection using the Helios Gate, then destroy the limiter that controls a Gate's ability to open and close, they can prevent that connection from being closed and the Void Wraith won't be able to make a connection to Theras Prime. Of course they pull it off, because heroes. The bomb blows up the Ghantan system, plus the sun Nolan connects to.

This strands Nolan until he and his crew can reach another Helios Gate, which will take four months. Nolan also deals with Edwards. It turns out Judicators are made from people, and Edwards can be turned into one. If he isn't, he'll probably die. Nolan orders him made into an Alpha Judicator, because, really, if you were going to be one wouldn't you want to be the twelve-foot-tall one with massive cannons? Hell, yes.

In the epilogue, we check in with Dryker, because there's one final question remaining for the reader: was I enough of a dick to kill Khar? No. Khar lives! The Primo rescue Dryker and Khar.

The End.

Ready to find out what happens next?

PROLOGUE

"Fall back to the choke point," Nolan bellowed, diving into cover behind the blue bulkhead. Plasma fire echoed up the corridor he'd come from, splashing against the edge of the doorway with a hot hiss.

Hannan was already moving, her retreating form disappearing up the stairs and into the room they'd chosen to make their stand in. Nolan staggered back to his feet, pounding up the stairs after her. He risked a glance behind him, catching sight of two Judicators stepping through the doorway.

Nolan redoubled his pace, leaping up the stairs three at a time until he crested the landing. The room ahead was full of alien equipment, but otherwise looked empty. That drew a half smile. If this was going to work, the enemy had to believe they had him and his squad on the run. Nolan went into a slide, rolling behind a robotic assembly arm. He sucked in greedy lungfuls of air, wiping sweat from his eyes.

"Contact," Hannan yelled from across the room. She was crouched behind a stack of crates containing parts for constructing Judicators. The soft lights set in the ceiling glinted off her bare scalp, painting her features with a deter-mined brush.

Nolan gripped his plasma rifle in both hands, taking aim at the top of the stairwell. Just in time. Three Judicators prowled into the room, their plasma rifles sweeping slowly back and forth as they sought targets. He resisted the urge to give the order to fire. Not yet.

Two more Judicators joined the first three, and all five began fanning out across the room. Nolan paused one moment longer. Should he wait to see if they could draw more into the trap? No, that was too risky. They needed to deal with them now, even if they didn't catch them all.

"Now!" Nolan barked.

He leaned out of cover, just far enough to begin firing. The plasma rifle vibrated, and a ball of shimmering blue plasma shot from the muzzle. The weapon was quite unlike standard UFC weaponry. There was no kick, and no maga-zine to swap out. It had a battery capable of generating dozens of shots before it needed to be recharged or replaced.

Nolan's shot took the lead Judicator in the face, picking it up and hurling it back down the stairs. It tumbled out of sight with a thunderous crash, but the others were already firing. Nolan ducked hastily behind cover, conscious of the robotic assembly heating up from repeated plasma shots.

Then Hannan burst from cover. She fired two quick bursts, each downing one of the Judicators. The remaining two tried to take aim at her, but she was already behind cover again. Nolan smiled grimly, lining up a shot on the first one. He squeezed the trigger, and his shot caught the Judicator in the midsection. It went down, leaving only one target.

"Clever," a voice whispered from above.

Nolan jerked erect, trying to bring up the barrel of his rifle. He was conscious of something falling toward him, and caught sight of golden fur as Fizgig knocked him to the deck. His rifle skittered away across the floor, and Nolan reached immediately for his sidearm. The plasma pistols were less powerful, but still nasty in close quarters.

"Don't," Fizgig said, placing a humming plasma blade against his throat. The blade extended from a blue metal bracelet wrapped around her wrist.

"I yield," Nolan said, uttering the ritual Tigris words with a sigh.

"Your confidence—" Fizgig began.

A volley of plasma came from the far side of the room as a twelve-foot-tall machine lurched into view. The Alpha Judicator let out burst after burst of plasma. The first caught Fizgig in the chest, hurling her off him and into the robotic assembly. The second caught Izzy, who was peeking over the stairs. The third took out the last of the Judicators.

"—is well placed, apparently. Nice work, Edwards," Nolan said, rolling to his feet with grin. He walked over to Fizgig, offering her a hand. Her fur stood on end, like she'd put her tail in a light socket.

Edwards lumbered closer, the massive Alpha stepping daintily between crates.

"Your confidence," Fizgig said again, as if he hadn't spoken, "borders on arrogance. I am disappointed, Nolan." Her tail swished back and forth, expressing her agitation.

"We won," Nolan said, resting the barrel of his rifle against his shoulder. "Isn't that what counts?"

"Did you?" Fizgig said, a low growl coming from deep in her chest. It was damned unnerving, and Nolan had to resist taking a step backward. "You led a single enemy squad into a trap, and while you successfully executed the trap, you

sacrificed *your* life to do it. If this was war—a real war—
what would your troops do now? You are dead. Would
Hannan take over? Is she capable of leading your forces?"

"I'm just a squad leader, not a captain," Hannan said,
rolling her shoulder experimentally as she approached.
"Damn, that shot I took from Izzy earlier really stings."

Izzy had crept back up the landing, though she looked
more than a little worse for wear. Her white fur had puffed
out from the plasma shot, and she looked more comical
than lethal. Nolan tried not to laugh. Despite Fizgig dressing
him down, he was proud of his victory.

"Maybe you're right, but this was just a scenario. Not a
real battle. In a real battle I shouldn't be commanding a
squad anyway. That's Hannan's turf," Nolan protested,
meeting Fizgig's feline gaze.

"There you are wrong," Fizgig said, showing an ample
supply of fangs. "A commander commands. It does not
matter if she is commanding infantry, or a starship. You
must be adaptable, and you cannot sacrifice yourself for
short-term goals."

"I haven't been trained for that," Nolan said, sighing.
"We're not Tigris, Fizgig. I'm not a bad shot, but I'll never be
able to fight like Hannan."

"Never?" Fizgig asked, her gaze smoldering. She took a
pace closer to Nolan. "You are intelligent, determined, and a
fast learner. You *can* learn to fight. You *must* learn to fight.
Do you know why we so easily overcame humanity during
the Eight-Year War, Nolan?"

"Because you had superior technology," Nolan replied
immediately. It was the line often given by UFC command.

"No," Fizgig snapped. "We won because we adapted. We
won because we are willing to learn new technology." She
ignited the plasma blade on her wrist, raising it to show

Nolan. "I had never even seen one of these until a few days ago, yet already I am proficient in its use. Why have you not picked one up?"

Nolan was silent for a long moment. Her words struck him like a physical blow. "You're right. Clearly I'm operating from the conventions I was trained under. I'm limiting myself."

"I'm glad you can see reason," Fizgig said. Her tail stopped swishing, and she smiled.

"We have—" Nolan checked his chronometer; his resolve firmed. "—eighty-one days before we reach a Helios Gate. Starting today, I want you to train me for an hour a day with one of those plasma blades. We'll spend another two hours drilling squad tactics, like today. Afternoons will be tactical theory."

"What of me, Captain?" Lena said, creeping cautiously over the stairs. "I'd like to be included in this combat training, yet I must also have time for my studies. We possess both the Primo VI and the one commandeered from the Void Wraith."

"Your top priority should be data parsing those," Nolan said, using his forearm to wipe sweat from his forehead. "It would be good to get you combat experience, but the things you discover could determine whether or not we win this war with the Void Wraith. They've got a three-month head start on us. I need you to balance that."

"Yes, mighty Nolan," she said, nodding deferentially. It was new, at least from her. The haughtiness was still there, but it was tempered by respect now.

The next few months were going to be hellish, and Nolan knew it. Not the training—*that*, he looked forward to —but the wondering. What were the Void Wraith up to?

1

81 DAYS LATER

The last three months had been hellish. Dryker gripped the curved railing, peering out the *First Light's* transparent dome. The Primo carrier provided a gorgeous view: an ever-growing fleet of massive warships orbiting a beautiful blue world. It was also mind-numbingly boring, because he'd seen the same view for the past eighty-one days, ever since they'd been rescued by the Primo.

"Another three carriers arrived during the night," Khar growled, joining him at the railing. The Tigris was back in fighting form, though he had several new scars from their last encounter with the Void Wraith. The most notable was a twelve-inch patch of white fur across his chest. Khar's tail lashed back and forth, and his eyes narrowed as he stared out at the fleet. His mane added to his height, and he towered over Dryker.

"I'll have Juliard catalogue them," Dryker said, listlessly. Juliard's arm had healed, and she'd thrown herself into data management. That meant reviewing both the data core he'd taken from the *Johnston* just before she'd blown up, and everything they'd learned during their months with the Primo. The latter was, regrettably, scarce. The Primo were tight-lipped, and Dryker still had little idea what was happening between the Tigris and humanity.

"I do not understand how gathering such data will be useful," Khar rumbled, resting his elbows on the railing as he studied the Primo home world. "If the Primo continue to imprison us, how will we tell anyone? How will we stop the war that has erupted between our peoples?"

Dryker clenched a fist, turning away from the Primo fleet. "We won't. But what else can we do? They're not going to release us until they're ready, and knowing the Primo we could die of old age first."

Cloth swished as Celendra, the Primo commander, approached. She was shorter than the imposing escorts that flanked her, though still taller than Dryker. Celendra walked with the odd reverse gait of her people—Primo legs bent in the opposite direction from a human's. Her skin was the color of seafoam, and her eyes were pools of deep red. She wore shimmering white garments, quite unlike most of the other Primo they'd met.

She slowed as she approached, her lantern eyes fixed on Dryker.

"You seem perturbed, Captain," Celendra said in a monotone characteristic of her species. "What has upset you this time?"

"This time?" Dryker said, suppressing the fire that bubbled up in his belly. "It's the same problem, Celendra. You've kept us here as 'guests' while our respective races go to war. Human and Tigris are wiping each other out, and Khar and I might be able to stop that if you'd let us return. You've seen the evidence I'm carrying."

"You lesser races are so impatient," Celendra said,

shaking her head sadly. She leaned on her staff, staring through the dome at the Primo fleet. "The last of us will arrive soon. We are so few now. Once they are here, we will begin the conclave. Your evidence will be central to our decision, and we need you here to deliver that. That must take precedence."

"What of our people?" Khar growled, his feline eyes narrowing to slits. "Do you care nothing for them? The war with the Void Wraith affects us all, and my people burn while you sit here in orbit doing nothing."

"Take care with your accusations, Tigris," Celendra said, somehow conveying menace with her flat tone. "As I've told you both repeatedly, we are not 'doing nothing.' It takes time to gather a conclave. If you are truly correct about the Void Wraith controlling the leadership of both your peoples, then the situation must be approached carefully. Our only advantage is surprise, and if we reveal our knowledge too soon our enemies will counter any moves we make."

"We may have already revealed that knowledge," Dryker countered. He took a step closer to the Primo, staring up fixedly at the taller alien. The Primo's skin glistened under the soft light. "I've warned you that your own race has likely been infiltrated as well. I even brought the first piece of proof. How else do you explain the attack on your own library by Primo forces?"

"I have no explanation as of yet, and it is possible we've been infiltrated," Celendra answered. Her words were clipped, and if Dryker hadn't known better he'd have said the Primo was furious.

"If your forces have been infiltrated, then the Void Wraith know about this conclave. You've got to realize that," Dryker said, trying one last time to appeal to the Primo's reason. "The *Claw of Tigrana* has been prepared. Let Khar and me go back to our people. We can try to stop this war. You have to know, the more allies we can gather, the better the chance we'll survive this."

"The conclave is nearly ready," Celendra said. She leaned closer to Dryker. "I have endured your tantrums, and humored your constant questions. I have been tolerant. That ends today. Do not ask me for your release again, or it may never come."

"Fine, don't release us. But at least move the conclave. Or do it over Quantum," Dryker pleaded, gesturing at the fleet orbiting the planet. "Can't you see that gathering your forces in one location is dangerous?"

Celendra didn't reply. She spun on her heel, stalking away. Dryker and Khar looked at each other, and all Dryker could do was sigh.

2

THE EYE

Delta had grown used to being ignored. It was an odd adjustment, because one didn't typically ignore combat-hardened officers—especially ones as tall and heavily muscled as he was. Add in his cybernetic arms, and he was generally the most threatening thing in any room.

Yet neither of the two people seated at the *Sparhawk*'s mess table seemed aware of his existence. Both were fixed on the holoprojector built into the center of the table. It projected a clean, high-definition image of their most illustrious ally, Admiral Mendez.

"Why have you contacted me, Reid?" Mendez leaned forward, spearing the pale-skinned doctor with his gaze. He puffed from a cigar burned down to one stubby end, a bit of ash tumbling from the tip.

"The Eye has arrived," Reid said, his pockmarked face splitting into a truly ghastly grin. "You know what that means, don't you?"

The admiral was silent, staring hard at Reid.

Delta glanced at the other figure at the table, Kathryn

Mendez. Her curly hair had been gathered into a severe ponytail, and her face was an emotionless mask. Such a change from when he'd first encountered her and Nolan. Delta leaned back against the wall, folding his metal arms together, and faded comfortably into the background.

The motion drew the admiral's attention. The older man sized Delta up in a single glance, then looked back to Reid. "I know what it means. I know that you stand higher than me, but I also know that my role is pivotal. I started the war between the humans and the Tigris, and it's my work that's causing that war to be so costly to both sides."

The words were defensive, and Reid's smile broadened. Delta had seen similar exchanges. Each time the admiral lost ground. Delta didn't know what the battle signified, or what they worked for. At least he'd pieced out that it *was* a what and not a who.

"Of course, Admiral," Reid said, wearing his smugness like a scarf. "I wasn't intending to disparage your excellent work, just reminding you that my own work is far more important. I will be journeying to meet the Eye, and I'll likely return with new orders. In the meantime, do you have any word about Nolan's return?"

"None," Mendez said, setting the remains of his cigar in a purple ashtray. The hologram was intricate enough to show a tiny streamer of smoke still rising from the ashes. "We're fairly certain he survived the explosion, but that's all. Kathryn, have any of the drops you've set up been triggered?"

The admiral's hologram turned to Kathryn, who straightened under the attention. She licked her lips before speaking. "No. I'm fairly certain he'd contact me if he was able to, which suggests he hasn't reached a Gate yet.

Depending on where he ended up, it could be years before he reaches one."

"Let's hope so," Mendez said, steepling his fingers. "He's proven entirely too disruptive. If he resurfaces, dealing with him should be our top priority."

Delta noted the shift in language. Before, the admiral would have said *will* be our top priority.

"If he resurfaces, I do not want him killed," Reid commanded. He brushed his stringy hair from his face, adjusting his glasses. "He would make an excellent host, and having him support our version of events would add fuel to the fire between the Tigris and the humans. Nolan must be implanted."

Delta shuddered. He loathed the chip in his brain, the one that controlled his actions and had even stripped his name from him. But at least it hadn't rewritten his DNA the way the larvae had Reid's, Kathryn's, and even the admiral's. Delta had no idea what the creatures did, but Reid looked a damned sight worse than he had when he and Delta had first met. Delta had a feeling the larvae weren't too good for the long-term health of the host.

"I don't like it," the admiral said, scowling. "He should be eliminated, ideally from both range and stealth. Nolan is smart, and he's entirely too resourceful. If we have the shot, we should take it."

"Leave Nolan to me," Reid said, giving another skeletal grin. "Or rather, leave him to your daughter. We have the perfect bait, Mendez, and I *will* use it."

3

HOME AGAIN

Nolan ducked low, touching the deck with his knee. Fizgig's plasma blade hummed through the space his neck had just occupied, and for a split second she was overextended. He jabbed upwards with his own plasma blade, the wrist-mounted weapon humming as it plunged into Fizgig's belly. Elation surged through him. Three months of hard work was paying off.

The elation was short-lived. Fizgig recovered, one furred paw grabbing his wrist, while the other rammed her plasma blade into his forehead. A familiar shock shot through his entire body, and he collapsed limply to the deck, twitching like a fish. His muscles refused to obey him, and blinding pain jetted down the right side of his body.

"Jeezzus," Nolan slurred, panting in quick little breaths. He shook his head to clear it, then clawed back to his feet, blinking away spots as the odd sensation faded. He was sweating profusely now. "I can't imagine these weapons at full strength."

It was hard to believe the lowest setting could be so powerful, but it did make them ideal for training. As Fizgig had pointed out early in their sparring, the shock taught students to fear the blade without making it lethal. Add to that the fact that they could be run continuously for several days without recharging, and when not in use could be worn decoratively, and you had a near-perfect weapon.

Almost as if to punctuate his final thought, Fizgig lifted her blade; it winked out, leaving nothing but a blue metallic ring around her wrist. It was covered in tiny golden circuitry, somehow managing to be both beautiful and intimidating. "They are indeed impressive," she said.

"And perfect for ramming into my face, apparently," Nolan said, rubbing his forehead. He extinguished his own blade. "At least I landed a blow that time."

"Yes," Fizgig replied, blinking. Her irises narrowed to slits. "I must admit I'm impressed with your progress. You've become competent at hand-to-hand, though you still have much to learn. Give me another year, and your name will strike fear amongst your enemies. As it is, you are no longer a danger to yourself. Now you must become a danger to others."

"Thanks," Nolan said, sardonically. He moved to the side of the makeshift sparring ring, picking up the piece of greasy fabric he'd been using as a towel. The Void Wraith ship was incredibly powerful, but it hadn't been designed with human comfort in mind. They'd had to improvise almost everything they needed to survive. "Shall we head up to the bridge for the strategy meeting?"

"I will meet you there," Fizgig said, licking the fur on her palm and using it to bathe the patch of white fur under her chin. "I'd like to finish grooming first."

Nolan nodded, turning from Fizgig and making his way toward the bridge. In the months they'd been here, he'd come to know their stolen harvester-class ship well, though it still felt like there were an infinite number of things to learn. He passed through the Judicator assembly room, which had thankfully gone silent when he'd ordered Ship to turn it off.

That left them with those Judicators who'd survived their taking of the harvester, a little over two dozen robotic minions. Unlike Edwards, they seemed completely emotionless. Each responded to commands, but they seemed incapable of independent thought beyond following the orders they'd been given.

Nolan trotted up the last stairwell, pleased to note that he wasn't winded from either the sparring match or the trek here. He was in much better physical shape now. They all were. Fizgig had been right, as usual.

Most of the others were already there when he arrived. Hannan lounged against the bridge's far wall, chatting quietly with Izzy. Oddly, the two had struck up quite a friendship during their journey. Or maybe not so oddly. They were both soldiers fighting on the front lines of the same war, after all.

Edwards hunched in a corner, not too far from them. His robotic blue face swiveled to face Nolan, those lantern eyes sizing him up. "Good morning, Commander. Uh, I mean Captain."

The voice was one hundred percent Edwards, which never failed to make Nolan smile. It was so odd hearing a plain-talking Marine's voice coming out of that massive robotic machine. The Alpha Judicators were a walking arsenal. A wall of blue death. Having Edwards inhabit one was going to be a wonderful ace in the hole when they reentered the war.

"Morning, Edwards. What's the good word?" Nolan asked. He'd picked up the greeting from Edwards.

"The word is *home*," Edwards said, straightening. Nolan could hear the smile in his voice. "Ship says that we're going to reach the Helios Gate today."

"About time," Hannan said, speaking up. She and Izzy were both looking at Nolan. "How'd the sparring go?"

"Fizgig disemboweled him. Again," Izzy said, waving a paw in Nolan's direction. She gave a fanged smile. "Better you than I. I've no wish to tangle with Fizgig. She terrifies me."

"Actually, this time *I* disemboweled *her*," Nolan said, aware that he'd let a little pride leak into his tone.

"Seriously?" Hannan asked. Izzy just gaped at him.

"I still lost the fight," Nolan explained, grinning. "But I managed to plant my blade in her gut. I'd be dead, but she'd be bleeding out, too. I'd call that a tie."

"That's a first," Hannan said, giving a low whistle. "Outside of Mills, I was the best hand-to-hand fighter in the squad, and I'm not sure I could take her."

"Let's hope we never have to find out which of us would win," Fizgig said, striding onto the bridge. She gave Hannan a respectful nod.

Lena followed closely after. Both Tigris had golden fur, and strongly resembled Earth's lions. Lena carried herself differently, though. She was more prim, more reserved. She also lacked Fizgig's jet-black armor, instead wearing the same simple white garments she'd had on when Nolan had met her.

"Captain," Lena said, giving a regal nod. She sank gracefully into one of the angular metal chairs they'd created in the machine shop.

"Morning, everyone," Nolan said, taking in the lot of them. He'd grown more comfortable with command over the last few months. It had become routine, though of course he hadn't really been tested since the last battle with the Void Wraith. "Today is a big day. We're going through the Helios Gate, and we're finally going to find out what's been happening since we left."

"Are you finally ready to share your plans?" Fizgig asked. She slowly folded her arms, her tail swishing gently behind her.

"I am," Nolan said, nodding. "We're going to stop by a human mining station, Coronas 6. I know the overseer, and I think he'll loan us a quantum transmitter. That will allow us to tap into the Quantum Network, so we can start catching up on everything we've missed."

4

HELIOS GATE

Nolan watched in awe as the harvester dove into the sun's corona. Their speed slowed, despite the tremendous gravity pulling them closer to the star. The vessel's inductive field sprang up around them, a ripple of faint blue energy that faded to invisibility after it formed. It was far more efficient than the human equivalent, using the star's own magnetic fields to sustain itself. The stronger they grew, the stronger the shield became.

They dove lower, and the holomap became an undulating mass of reds, whites, and blues. "Ship, raise the temperature band we're monitoring."

"Of course, Captain," Ship said, cheerfully. Nolan thought of the Primo VI that way—as though "Ship" were its proper name—now that it had merged with the Harvester. They all did. After all, they couldn't keep calling it "Primo Virtual Intelligence" every time they spoke to or about it.

Of course, they probably couldn't go on just calling it "Ship" either. But they had more important things to worry about.

The hologram shifted, showing the sun's interior—a soup of charged particles so dense they distorted magnetic fields like a cat playing with yarn.

"Seeing the inside of a star makes me uneasy," Lena said, seizing her tail in both hands. Her eyes were wide, reflecting the light of the hologram.

"Doesn't bother me," Nolan shrugged. "I have to admit, I take Helios travel for granted. We've had it since I was a kid."

Lena shot him a look that made it clear he'd insulted her. "We've had it for generations, Captain," she said. "I may only be an anthropologist, but all scientists learn multiple disciplines. Helios travel is one of mine, so I understand the implausibility of what we are doing. We're displacing the densest matter in the universe, using equations so complex that everything I understand about science tells me this should be impossible. Did you know that it can take light over a hundred thousand years to escape the core of a star?"

"Captain," Ship interrupted, its voice hesitant. "I've discovered something troubling. Something I hadn't noticed when we dove through the Gate in the Ghantan system."

"Go on," Nolan said, trying to be encouraging. He wasn't sure how human this thing was, but it acted as if it had emotions, so he tried to treat it like crew.

"This vessel can interface with the Helios Gate in ways unlike what was possible in my time," Ship said. "My preliminary scans of the *Johnston*'s inductive control module suggest your race does not have these interface capabilities either."

"Capabilities to do what?" Edwards asked, slapping the wall of the ship with one of his gigantic hands. "Spit it out, already."

"This vessel can issue a command to the Gate—a command that would cause the Gate to transform into a vessel, and give it travel instructions to another Gate," Ship said. "The language used is clearly Primo, yet this technology was unknown to my people. That is troubling. It suggests the possibility that something existed earlier, and that whatever came earlier created the Gates."

"An even earlier empire?" Lena said, blinking. She rose gracefully to her feet. "Ship, I'm heading to my quarters. Compile all information about these commands, and begin making a list of..." Her voice faded as she strode off the bridge.

"All right, everyone," Nolan said, smiling after Lena. "It's time to rejoin civilization. Real showers and hot meals, here we come."

CORONAS 6

"Hail them," Nolan ordered, watching the holographic display of the Coronas mining station.

It floated by itself, a tiny dot near a dense patch of asteroids clustered in an area the size of a moon. Little drones zipped to and from the station, their bright torches flaring as they carved hunks of ore from the asteroids.

"You have a live connection, Captain," Ship said, in its friendly monotone. They really needed to give it a name.

"Unidentified vessel, please state your intention," came a reedy voice. Evidently their request for a video connection had been denied.

"Hello, Bock," Nolan said. "It's been a while since I last saved your ass."

There was a long silence. Nolan knew Bock was remembering the attack on his mining station, an attack Nolan had helped fend off, back before his exile to the 14th.

"Nolan?" Bock's voice finally said. The fear was still there, but there was a little excitement in it, too.

"That's right. Listen, my crew and I have been on a long

trip," Nolan explained. He talked fast, knowing if he didn't there was a chance Bock would cut the connection. "We're just reentering the data stream. To do that I have to ask you a favor. I need to borrow a quantum transmitter. I know that's a big ask, but we can—"

"That transmitter is Coronas property. I can't give it up," Bock said.

"You realize we could simply take it, do you not, worm?" Fizgig growled from beside Nolan. "Listen, tiny human. I will squeeze the breath out of you myself, and devour your corpse whole. If—"

"Fizgig," Nolan snapped. The Tigris glared at him, her tail lashing back and forth. After a long, tense moment she averted her gaze. Nolan turned back to the comm. "I'm sorry about that, Bock. I should have mentioned that some of my friends are Tigris."

"Are you crazy?" Bock shrieked. "You have to leave. *Right now.* I can't have you anywhere near this station."

"Captain," Ship said. "The connection has been severed."

"Board them," Fizgig said, stalking up to Nolan. "We can take what we need. They cannot stop us."

"No, they can't," Nolan said, taking a half step toward Fizgig. They were inches apart now, but he forced himself to meet her gaze. She'd never respect him otherwise. "That isn't how we do things. These are my people, Fizgig, and I'm not going to steal their only method of communicating with the outside world. Not without their permission."

"Then what do you plan to do?" she growled. Her hackles stood on end now. Not a good sign.

Out of the corner of his eye, Nolan saw Hannan wrap her hand around the grip of her sidearm. He could tell from her stance that she was ready to take Fizgig down if needed.

"We're going to board their ship, pay them for the supplies we buy, and use their transmitter. We don't need to steal it. We can spend a few hours gathering the data we need, then leave the system. We'll find another transmitter," Nolan said. He leaned in even closer, close enough to smell Fizgig's fetid breath. "No one dies. No one is even harmed. Not without cause. We need these people's goodwill, Fizgig. And we have a larger problem."

"What problem?" Fizgig asked. Her tone softened, and her tail slowed.

"You heard the way Bock reacted to us having Tigris on board," Nolan said. "He sounded terrified. Something has changed since we left, and I want to know what it is. We need him to cooperate, and you terrifying him isn't going to make that happen."

Fizgig was silent. Then she gave a single nod. "Apologies, Captain Nolan. I have overstepped my place. I am used to bearing the burden of command. This subservience...I am ill-suited to it. I will remain on the ship with Izzy and Lena."

"Apology accepted. Ship, dock with the station. Hannan, you're with me. The rest of you, stay put," Nolan ordered.

6

CATCHING UP

Hannan followed Nolan to the airlock, using the time to consider as they made their way through the ship. She liked the direction Nolan was going. He was less reticent about command, and seemed to have found his confidence. That confidence had been lacking when he'd been assigned to the *Johnston*, though that was true for most officers in the 14th. Everyone knew it was a death sentence for your career.

"What can we expect inside, sir?" Hannan asked. Nolan didn't demand the honorific, but she made sure to always use it. It set a good example, one that Edwards followed. Nolan was in charge, and Hannan wanted to make sure the cats saw that. Especially Fizgig, who had a real problem remembering she wasn't their leader.

"A warm welcome, I'm hoping. They don't have much in the way of firearms—and, besides, these people owe me," Nolan said, striding up to the airlock door. He tapped the red button, turning to face her as it went green. "Bock is a bit of a weasel, but he'll work with us as long as we don't take or damage Coronas property."

Hannan relaxed a hair, but only a hair. The captain wasn't expecting trouble, but it was her *job* to expect it. She watched as the airlock door slid open, then she followed the captain inside. She kept her hand close enough to grab her sidearm if necessary, but not so close the station personnel would find it threatening.

The door slid closed behind them, and there was a brief hiss. Then the door leading into the station slid open. A crowd of people milled about outside the airlock, and some were trying to press inside. Most had their hands full, with everything from soy cakes to a bottle of wine with a bow tied around it. Hannan's weapon was in her hand and snapped into a firing position before she could even think.

"Stand back!" she barked in her best parade voice.

The people nearest the door tried to fall back, but those behind them continued to push. Hannan glanced at Nolan, but before she could receive instructions a shrill whistle killed the cacophony.

"Every one of you grease-swilling mongrels, listen up," a female voice boomed through the station. "Commander Nolan's got business with Bock, not the likes of you. Give the man some room. He ain't here for a goddamned party."

The crowd immediately began to disperse, most of the people retreating to other airlock doors. Hannan holstered her sidearm, but she stepped protectively ahead of Nolan, scanning for threats. The only potential target was the woman who'd spoken. She stood at the top of a wide stair-well that ascended toward what appeared to be an office.

The woman wore stained grey overalls, and had a pump-action shotgun absently propped over one shoulder. She stared impassively down at Hannan, meeting her gaze without flinching.

"Annie, it is damned good to see you," Nolan said, trotting up the stairs to meet her. He took the woman's hand, giving her a huge smile.

Hannan trotted after the commander, sizing Annie up as she approached. Her voice screamed NCO, but Hannan didn't peg her for a Marine.

"You served?" Hannan asked, nodding at Annie.

"11th infantry," the woman said, releasing Nolan's hand and offering hers to Hannan.

Hannan took it.

"Marine?" Annie asked. "Don't often see you types out of uniform."

"We've been through it," Hannan said, giving Annie a smile. She found herself liking the woman.

"Annie, this is Sergeant Hannan. She's kept my ass alive for the last few months, not an easy task," Nolan said, half-turning toward the office at the top of the stairs.

"Last I checked you were on a little speck of a vessel. The *Sparhawk*? With that lady you were making eyes at. Kathryn, right?" Annie said.

"We've got a lot to catch up on, but not much time to do it," Nolan said, looking uncomfortable.

Nolan hadn't spoken much about his past, but Hannan knew the stories. Kathryn must be Commander Mendez, the admiral's daughter. "I need to talk to Bock."

"He's up there in his office. I stood guard to make sure he didn't try running off," Annie said, giving a grin. Her teeth were stained from tobacco. "Head on in. He's expecting you. I'll keep your friend here company."

"You want me to wait here, sir?" Hannan asked, raising an eyebrow. Since he'd started training with Fizgig, Nolan was far more capable of taking care of himself. She still didn't like the idea of him being alone with an unknown, but he called the shots.

"Do that," Nolan nodded. He shook Annie's hand. "We'll catch up soon."

Then Nolan trotted up the stairs and into the office.

7
———

BOCK AND NOLAN

Nolan ducked into the tiny office, a wash of memories flowing over him. Last time he'd come here it had been with Kathryn. They'd led a last-ditch defense against Delta, a cybernetically enhanced UFC soldier working for Admiral Chu. They'd won that fight, but the victory had been short-lived.

He dropped into the seat across from a weaselly-looking man he had never expected to see again. Bock's eyes darted about, like those of a panicked animal looking for a direction to flee.

"Hello, Bock," Nolan said. He rested his elbows on the narrow desk, fixing the administrator with his best officer's gaze. "You have information I need. You also have a quantum transmitter, and I need access to it."

Then Nolan leaned back, waiting. He knew this would be a negotiation; the more he gave, the harder the price Bock would demand. So he let the silence stretch, waiting for Bock to respond.

"All right," Bock said, licking his lips. His eyes were wide, but a hint of greed now lit them. "What do I get out of this?"

"That's a good question," Nolan said. "It really depends on what I get. You saw my ship. You know you're not in much of a bargaining position."

"Maybe not, but you're an officer of the UFC," Bock said. His eyes narrowed and he gave a predatory smile. "An officer who deserted in a time of war. An officer consorting with the enemy. One Quantum call and I could inform the admiralty."

Nolan was silent for a long time, considering Bock's words. They'd knocked him back a half step mentally. "Consorting with the enemy? What the hell does that mean?"

"Are you serious?" Bock asked, his surprise genuine. He blinked several times. "We're at war with the Tigris. They're crushing us. Where the hell have you been?"

Nolan took a deep breath, ignoring the question. The wheels began turning in his head, and when he realized what had likely happened he felt physically ill. Admiral Mendez was almost certainly behind this. He was a masterful strategist, and even though Nolan had blown up his fleet and his factory, the admiral had still managed to turn events to his advantage.

"How and when did the war start?" Nolan asked, though he was fairly sure he already knew the answers.

"Wow, you really *have* been out of it," Bock said, cunningness suddenly shading his features. "Listen, I can catch you up, but I'm going to want a few things. How about you give me the specs for the ship you're flying, and I'll bring you up to speed? I'll even let you use the transmitter, and you can have half off on docking fees."

"Bock," Nolan said, leaning across the desk until he was staring directly into the administrator's tiny little eyes. "You're going to tell me all about this war, *right now*. Then you're going to let me use the transmitter. If you're right about me being AWOL, you realize what that makes me, right?"

"A—a pirate?" Bock asked, eyes widening in realization.

"Now, why don't you tell me about this war?" Nolan said, sliding back into his seat. He stared fixedly at Bock, watching the administrator squirm.

"Okay," Bock said, sighing. "It started about three months ago. The Tigris claimed that we blew up one of their science vessels, and they sent a fleet to hunt down the ship that did it. A destroyer by the name of the *Johnston*, I think. Anyway, the Tigris fleet caught up to the *Johnston* at the same time as the 7th fleet. There was a big battle, and the 7th was wiped out. The Tigris claim we started the war, and started attacking our outlying systems."

"What about the Primo? Have they reacted to the war?" Nolan asked. The Primo actively discouraged large-scale warfare, and it had been their intervention that had brought the Eight-Year War to an early close.

"They haven't. In fact, no one has seen a Primo vessel in months," Bock said, shrugging. "Not that anyone can figure out why the Primo do anything. They're probably worshipping some nebula somewhere, praying to God knows what."

"How has the war progressed?" Nolan asked, straightening in the chair. He could feel his shoulders tensing, like they were preparing for a blow.

"Not well," Bock said, his face softening into something like pity. "We're outclassed. There've been a couple victories, but we've lost the bulk of several fleets. If something doesn't change, the Tigris will reach Earth in a few more months."

"Damn it," Nolan muttered, clenching a fist. It was as bad as he'd expected. Worse maybe. If humans and Tigris ground down their respective militaries, it would make it easier for the Void Wraith to sweep in and wipe out both races. It was brilliantly executed. "Bock, I need the Quantum Network. Right now."

If anyone knew the lay of the land, it would be Kathryn. He'd start there.

8

ARRANGE IT

Delta's eyes snapped open, but he remained lying down. He watched as Kathryn dropped lightly to the deck from the bunk above his. The bunks were set into the ship's bulkhead, and were just wide enough for an adult to sleep on the neurofoam pads. It was comfortable, especially for a frigate this size. Four people could comfortably live aboard the *Sparhawk*, with most of the creature comforts afforded by a capital ship.

"Reid, wake up," Kathryn demanded. She leaned across the aisle, shaking the skinny doctor awake. Delta noticed the sour cast to her features when she touched the man. It was reassuring to know he wasn't the only one who found Reid repulsive.

"Stop touching me, woman," Reid snapped, recoiling to the corner of his bunk. "I'm awake. What do you want?"

"Nolan contacted me," Kathryn said, holding up her comm. Her eyes were still murky from sleep, but her voice was clear. "He's requested a meeting. As soon as possible."

"Fine," Reid snapped, swinging his legs from the bunk. "Now go pilot the ship or something. I need room to get up."

Kathryn merely nodded, walking up the narrow corridor to the *Sparhawk*'s mess. Delta didn't exactly pretend to be asleep; he just laid there listening as Reid got up. The doctor was out of breath by the time he got to his feet, and he wove unsteadily into the mess. A thick sheen of sweat covered his brow, and there was something off about the color of that sweat. Instead of clear, it was a murky green.

Delta watched him carefully, considering. Reid's health had been bad when they'd first met, but it was getting worse, and the process seemed to be accelerating. That prompted some interesting questions. He didn't know what had been done to Reid—or to Kathryn, for that matter—but whatever it was seemed to have long-term ill effects.

"Delta, get in here," Reid called, half turning from the bench to start a cup of coffee.

Delta didn't reply, just rose soundlessly and headed into the mess. He sat at the very corner of the table, as far from Reid as he could get. Kathryn was seated similarly, at the opposite corner of the bench on the same side as Delta.

"Tell me," Reid demanded, looking hard at Kathryn.

"Nolan read the messages I've been leaving him," Kathryn explained, sliding her comm across the table to Reid. "That's the answer he sent. He's back, and he'd like a face-to-face."

"Excellent," Reid said, delivering a truly ghastly smile. "Arrange the meeting."

"Should we alert my father?" Kathryn asked, raising an eyebrow. "Nolan is no fool, and if reports from the final battle are accurate he's in possession of a Void Wraith vessel."

"I said arrange the meeting," Reid said, eyes narrowing. The smile vanished. "Delta is more than capable of dealing with the situation. Even if he were not, we have the toys he's been provided. Their enhancements make them more than a match for any crew Nolan might have surrounded himself with."

"Okay, I'll arrange it," Kathryn said. Her tone made it clear how she felt about it, and Delta privately agreed with her. Nolan was resourceful, and underestimating him wasn't smart.

9

ANNIE

There was an awkward silence as Hannan watched Annie, and Annie watched Hannan. The rest of the crowd had dispersed, and Nolan had disappeared into the office with Administrator Bock. Hannan studied the dirty miner, impressed by what she saw. Soot covered Annie's crow's feet, and Hannan was positive there were callouses under those thick leather gloves. Annie worked for a living, that much was clear.

Annie withdrew a rusty tin from her pocket, unscrewing the top and offering it to Hannan. It smelled of pungent tobacco, something Hannan had never gotten into. A lot of soldiers enjoyed it, but it was expensive and messy.

"No, thanks," she said, shaking her head. "I'd kill for a beer, though, if you guys have anywhere that sells one. Maybe we can persuade the captain to stop for one after he's done."

"Captain?" Annie asked, withdrawing a pinch of tobacco and tucking it under her lip. "Last I checked Nolan was a commander. He didn't even have his own vessel, much less whatever the hell that beast you arrived in is."

"Yeah, a lot's changed since Nolan came on board the *Johnston*," Hannan said, glancing up the stairs at the office door. She considered guarding her tongue, but Nolan clearly trusted Annie, and she wasn't spilling state secrets or anything.

"You folks were on the *Johnston*?" Annie said. She got real interested, her eyes fixing Hannan. "Now there's a story I want to hear. The *Johnston* started the war with the Tigris, and the press ain't been too free with the particulars of how that happened. All we know is the 7th was wiped out, and took a fleet of cats with 'em."

Hannan blinked. She stayed silent a moment, considering. What the hell had been happening while they were gone? Had Mills made it? Dryker would have gotten him out, if it was possible.

The door at the top of the stairs opened, and Nolan strode down the stairs. His face was grim, his shoulders squared. That was a man carrying a whole load of new trouble, and given what Annie had just said, Hannan had a feeling she knew exactly what that trouble was.

"Sir?" she asked as Nolan approached.

"Bad news and worse news," Nolan said, sighing. "We'll discuss it on the ship. I hate to be rude, but we need to run, Annie. We're three months behind, and it sounds like we've got a hell of a lot to catch up on."

"Nolan, you've got to level with me," Annie said, folding her arms. "What the hell happened in the Ghantan system?"

"You saved my ass," Nolan said, giving Annie a wistful smile, "but I don't have time to get into specifics. The short version? The war between humanity and the Tigris is a con job. The people who made my current ship are trying to wipe us all out, and they figure the best way to do it is by having us do it to ourselves."

Annie blinked, then looked at the airlock door leading back to their vessel.

"Sir, you admit you owe me, right?" Annie said. "I did save your bacon."

"Of course," Nolan said, nodding. "I won't ever forget that, and if I'm in a position to help, I'll do whatever I can. I owe you."

"Well I'm calling in that marker, sir," Annie said. She tightened the grip on her shotgun, cocking it loudly. "I'm a soldier, and we got us a war on. Take me with you. I'm certain and a half that you're gonna be in the thick of it, and that whatever battle you're fighting is going to help decide the war."

Nolan was silent for a long moment, weighing Annie with that calculating gaze.

"Sir," Hannan said, clearing her throat. She leaned in to Nolan and lowered her voice. "We need the manpower, and it looks like she can handle herself."

Nolan met her gaze and nodded, then he turned to Annie. "All right, Annie, welcome aboard. We'll leave the docking bay open, just dock and we'll get the hell out of this system."

"Sure thing, sir," Annie said, giving a tobacco-stained smile. "Just got to make a quick stop, and I'll be right on over."

10

TIBS

Annie brushed empty cans and wrappers from the co-pilot's chair, dropping her new acquisition into the seat. It wouldn't do to show up empty-handed. Nolan had a new ship, and that meant she needed to bring a housewarming gift. She'd even paid for it, after a fashion.

Annie smiled as she began flicking switches on the console. Her shuttle's engine begrudgingly rumbled to life, sputtering periodically as it fought to maintain a more or less consistent power output. Bock had asked a pretty penny for the quantum transmitter. In the end she'd agreed to waive all the back payments he owed her. He'd said that wasn't enough, so she'd thrown in the fact that she wouldn't fill his face with buckshot. That had done the trick.

She waited a precise thirty seconds for the engine to reach equilibrium before tapping the docking release. It fired off a command to the station, which obligingly released her shuttle. It was the first time she'd actually left Coronas 6 in over two years. During that time, she'd lived on this shuttle, and the idea of changing that was more than a little scary. Didn't much matter, though. Fear wasn't something you could control, not really. You could only control how you reacted to it.

"This is Annie on the shuttle *Tibs*," Annie said into the comm. "Nolan, that beast of yours got a name?"

Annie guided her ponderous shuttle around the station, gaping openly when she got a good look at Nolan's vessel. It was massive, easily on par with the largest battleships ever produced by humanity. She thought it might even be larger than a Tigris vessel. The sleek wings tapered to sharp tips, and looked perfect for ramming enemy vessels. She didn't see any obvious weaponry, and wondered what kind of armament that thing packed.

"Shuttle *Tibs*, this is the Void Wraith harvester," a strange voice responded. It wasn't exactly female—or male, either. It was...alien. "As of this time this vessel has not received an official designation. I am currently referred to as Ship."

"Okay, Ship," Annie replied, guiding the *Tibs* in a wide arc that brought it below the harvester. "Looks to me like you've got a docking bay right there beneath the main section where the wings meet. That where you want me to go?"

"Affirmative," Ship replied. "There will be an escort waiting to meet you."

Annie watched the harvester get larger and larger, and blinked as she passed under the gigantic vessel. She'd been wrong. It would dwarf a Tigris ship. It might be as large as a Primo carrier, and so far as she knew that was the largest ship out there. Annie's tiny shuttle disappeared into a wide docking bay, which appeared to be all but empty. There were no other shuttles, just a stack of crates against one wall.

Annie landed the *Tibs*, which lurched to a halt atop the deck. She started flipping switches, shutting down the reactor and most of the secondary systems. They hadn't been used in a while, and every last one of them was due for maintenance. The *Tibs* was at least seventy-five percent duct tape, and that meant it wasn't wise to operate her any longer than was necessary.

Once the vessel was shut down Annie picked up the quantum transmitter, tucking it under her arm as she left the cockpit. She threaded between the walls of junk filling most of the *Tibs*'s cargo hold, using her free hand to tap the docking ramp. It slid slowly down, a hiss of pressure washing over her as the atmosphere normalized with the larger ship's.

With a curse, Annie darted back a step, yanking her spare shotgun from the wall holster. Damn her for not thinking like a soldier. Her weapon was in the cockpit. A soldier never left her weapon behind.

She leaned forward, aiming at the Tigris standing at the base of the ramp. The cat had long, snowy fur, dotted with black spots, but the cuddly part ended in sharp claws and long fangs.

"You're going to want to take a big step back from my shuttle, cat," Annie said, taking a step to the lip of the ramp. She had the cat in her crosshairs, and if that thing moved it was going to die.

"Okay," the Tigris said, taking a very large step back. It—she—blinked rapidly. "Is that far enough? I do not understand human customs."

"Annie," Hannan called from the doorway to the docking bay. She strode briskly toward the *Tibs*. "Put that gun down. You don't need it."

The Marine stopped next to the Tigris, wrapping an arm around her furry shoulder. "This is Izzy. Izzy's a good kitty."

"You know I hate it when you say that," Izzy said, elbowing Hannan in the ribs.

"Y'all got Tigris on your crew?" Annie said, raising her eyebrows. "This is going to be an interesting deployment."

11

LENA'S DISCOVERY

Lena turned on the acetylene torch she'd clamped to her makeshift table, setting the flask full of water on it to heat. She had no tea, of course, but she still completed the ritual. Teatime calmed her, even when it was just a mug of hot water. It was a practice she'd embraced since she was a kit, even before she'd gone to the Royal Academy to study Anthropology.

Once the water was tended to, Lena smoothed her flowing white pants, and sat primly atop the stool Edwards had made for her. She appreciated the human's desire to help, especially given his transformation. He was unfailingly respectful to her, always using the honorific *ma'am*. She didn't know what it meant, but could tell from the respectful tone that it denoted an elder of some kind.

"Ship, bring up the data file you flagged," Lena ordered, warming her paws over the fire. The ship wasn't precisely cold, but it was a few degrees cooler than she was used to. Tigris vessels ran hotter, and she liked it that way.

A holographic file appeared, text hovering on one side and graphics on the other. This bit showed a strand of DNA, the double helix that humans, Primo, and Tigris all shared. This particular bit belonged to not just any Primo, but to the earliest Primo found in the ship's data core. Lena scanned the text, eyes widening at the age. It was nearly forty thousand years old, older than the original empire she and Nolan had discovered back on Purito. Older by far.

"Ship, the article doesn't contrast this strand with a modern version. Can you sequence both sets of DNA, and give me a summary of the major differences?" Lena asked. She turned off the torch, blowing lightly across the flask as she waited for the water to cool.

"Processing," Ship said. The holographic representation disappeared, and Lena wrapped a paw experimentally around the flask. It was hot, but not too hot to pick up. She settled both paws around it, and raised it to her mouth for a tiny sip.

A moment later, a new hologram sprang into view. This one had two DNA strands, each very similar. Below them was a bulleted list of differences, and Lena could only blink as she read the summary. The implications of this discovery could not be overstated.

"Honored one?" came a quiet voice from the doorway. Lena looked up to see Izzy peering around the corner of the door. "It is time for the evening meal. Nolan sent me to fetch everyone."

"I'll be there shortly," Lena replied, waving absently at Izzy as she focused on the data.

12

BISCUITS

Nolan pulled out one of the uncomfortable metal chairs, sitting next to Hannan. Fizgig and Izzy sat across from them, while Edwards had squeezed his metallic body into the corner of their makeshift mess. Everything from the chairs to the table had been fabricated recently, as the ship hadn't been built to support human occupants. Thank God there was a machine shop.

"That smells amazing," he said, eyeing the pot of stew in the center of the table. High-rimmed metal plates sat in front of everyone, along with chromed glasses full of water.

"Wait until you taste these," Annie boomed, grinning as she approached the table. She wore a pair of oven mitts, and carried a tray of fist-sized biscuits. They smelled even better than the stew. "You don't have much in the way of cooking equipment, but we can use the *Tibs* until we get something rigged."

Annie set the tray of biscuits near the center of the table. Izzy stretched out a paw to snatch one, but Fizgig batted her paw away and gave her the kind of condescending look only Fizgig could manage.

"Where's Lena?" Nolan asked, not seeing her anywhere in the mess.

"She said she'd be here shortly, Mighty Nolan," Izzy said, though her gaze never left the biscuits. "She seemed very excited. I believe she found something important in the Primo data core."

"Will she be offended if we start without her?" Nolan asked, looking to Fizgig.

"She will not," Fizgig said, giving a half smile. "She might not show up at all. That one is a true scientist, one of our best. It consumes her."

"Let's dig in, then. Thank you for this, Annie. We've been surviving on protein paste for the past three months," Nolan said, ladling a generous portion of stew onto his plate. He passed the ladle to Hannan, who served up her own portion, then passed the ladle to Izzy.

"My pleasure. I love cooking," Annie said, cramming a biscuit into her mouth. She spoke around mouthfuls. "I ain't too civilized, but I can turn an old sock and some grease into a decent meal."

"Is that what they feed you infantry types? Old socks?" Edwards's voice came from the far side of the room, startling all of them. The tone was playful, but his sheer size was still intimidating.

"Jesus, is that thing alive?" Annie said, blinking. She picked up a second biscuit, absently chewing as she approached Edwards. "You some kind of robot? Doesn't look like UFC tech, any more than this ship does."

"I'm a...what did Lena call me? A *cybernetically enhanced life form*," Edwards said, offering Annie a massive blue hand. She grabbed his index finger and shook it.

The exchange made Nolan smile. Edwards had kept his distance during the long voyage home, though the longer they were out here the more he seemed to be adjusting.

"Captain," Lena said, breezing into the room. She sat daintily on the corner of the bench next to Izzy, her feline eyes alight with excitement. "I've discovered something monumental, something I think may be very important."

Nolan finished his biscuit, then offered Lena his full attention. She'd come to him during the trip home with several *monumental discoveries*, none of which were relevant to their situation—or all that monumental, in his opinion.

"What did you find?" he asked, scooping up something resembling a potato from the stew on his plate.

"I found an account from a Primo scientist. He was a citizen of the empire you and I discovered back on Purito, one who did groundbreaking work on genetics. He believed that his race had been genetically modified, but his ideas were dismissed as wild conspiracy theories," Lena said, leaning across the table. She licked her chops in a most alarming way, seemingly unaware of Hannan shrinking back from her. "He found markers indicative of tampering. He was certain of it. So he spent over forty years cataloguing Primo DNA, looking for blood stains, ancient sites, and anything else that might yield an intact genome. After many years he found it, a sample from a skeleton that was at least forty thousand years old." Lena paused, perhaps for dramatic effect. "This sample lacked the genetic markers found in modern Primo. By comparing the samples, the researcher realized that someone had deliberately altered the Primo, and that the alteration occurred somewhere between fifty and sixty thousand years ago."

"What does that mean?" Edwards asked. His metallic face turned in their direction.

"It means," Lena continued, shooting Edwards an

annoyed glance, "that someone bred the Primo, in the same way your species breeds dogs. Their markers encouraged specific traits—in this case, aggression and increased fertility."

"They were breeding soldiers," Nolan said, making the connection instantly. "This is further evidence. Look how the Void Wraith function. They depopulate worlds, and convert those they harvest into Judicators. It would make sense that they want those Judicators as lethal as possible. Why not modify the species you're abducting to have the traits you find most desirable?"

"I believe you're correct, but I think there's a greater revelation here," Lena said, positively beaming now. "If I'm correct, there are three distinct eras of Primo development. The one I am studying now isn't the first, as I'd originally assumed. There's an even earlier empire, probably the one that first encountered the Void Wraith. This reshapes tens of thousands of years of Primo history. Everything they believe about their origins is a lie. Their ancestors were space faring when mine were hunting monkans in the jungle."

"That's fascinating, Holy One," Fizgig allowed. She'd been using a claw to carefully spear chunks of meat from the stew, but was ignoring the rest of the food. "Yet, I am unsure why you consider this discovery so important."

"Because I don't believe the Void Wraith are the real enemy. Their weapons and ships are clearly of Primo design," Lena explained. "I believe that someone or something else showed up, turned the Primo's own citizens and weapons against them, and then harvested them into a massive army. When they were finished, they modified the remaining Primo to have their desired traits. Then they left."

"So you think these are literal harvests," Nolan said, understanding. "The Void Wraith, or whoever made the

Void Wraith, pop by every so-many-thousands of years to build another army."

"If that's the case, that's terrifying," Hannan said. "What the hell do you use an army that size for?"

"Lena, is it possible that this first group of Primo might have left behind a library? Some source of knowledge we can tap into to learn more?" Nolan asked. "If the war really is cyclic, we need to know as much as possible about it. If they're the ones who first encountered the Void Wraith, then they have the best chance of knowing what really happened."

"Very possible," Lena said, nodding. "Now that I know what to look for, I believe I might be able to learn more. We could do that at any of the oldest Primo libraries. One of their researchers could point us in the right direction. In the meantime, I'll study the early mythology in the current data core. It's possible there's more there. Myths and legends often hold a bit of literal truth."

13

DRYKER

Dryker shifted uncomfortably in his brand-new uniform. It fit perfectly, but it felt stiff and confining after spending the last few months in the flowing Primo garments they'd been provided. He had no idea where they'd gotten the uniform, either. Did the Primo just happen to have captain's bars on hand? It didn't really matter, he guessed.

"Are you ready, Dryker?" Khar boomed, flexing his claws as he approached. The Tigris had been given a full set of black war armor, and now carried a gleaming silver spear. The weapon was an ancestral favorite for the Tigris, used to kill fleeing prey. Fleeing humans, the last time Dryker had seen one used.

"As ready as I'll ever be," Dryker said, turning from the mirror and exiting the lavish quarters.

Juliard was already waiting in the hall, her face buried in her comm. The fact that they couldn't reach the Quantum Network didn't seem to phase her. She had a seemingly endless number of games, and was playing one of them now. She stopped at his approach, sliding her comm into her pocket.

"Sir," she said, nodding.

"Let's get this over with," Dryker said, walking down the corridor and into the ship's main chamber.

The *First Light*'s central chamber was an invention unique to the Primo. Human and Tigris vessels were both compact. They had only enough room for their crew to function, and no space was wasted. Even the most modern UFC ship used an economical design.

The Primo had taken the opposite route. The central chamber was cavernous, with a ceiling that vaulted several hundred feet into the air. Globes of energy dotted the ceiling, making the blue metallic walls sparkle. In the center of the room was a huge, flat disk. The center of that disk was slightly raised, and appeared just large enough for a single person to stand on.

The entire aft wall was transparent, a gigantic dome providing a spectacular view of space. Three golden thrones floated in the air near that dome, bobbing slowly up and down. Their occupants wore shimmering silver garments unlike anything Dryker had seen the others wear. Some sort of parade dress, probably. He recognized one of the three figures as Celendra, but the other two were unfamiliar.

Both were male—one with deep purple skin, the other a pallid grey. Celendra floated between them, though Dryker had no idea if that signified anything. He still had very little understanding of how Primo politics worked, which made them damnably difficult to navigate.

Below the chairs, several hundred Primo were gathered, more than he'd ever seen gathered in one place. Primo were powerful, but rare. They were secretive about their numbers, but he'd guess there couldn't be more than a hundred thousand remaining. Their colonies had long been abandoned, and they'd retreated all the way to Theras Prime, the world the *First Light* was currently orbiting.

"As the hosting navigator, I call this conclave to order. Endari of the *Fist of Endari* and Kayton of the *Rising Star* sit in witness," Celendra's clear voice echoed through the room as she gestured first at the grey-skinned Primo, and then the purple. Dryker realized the timing wasn't a coincidence, as she was staring in his direction. She must have been waiting for him before starting. "I have called this conclave to discuss the threat posed by the Void Wraith, and to decide how our people can best respond."

"I have still seen no evidence that these Void Wraith even exist," Endari said, eyeing Celendra sharply. His grey skin had a waxy look Dryker had seen on the oldest Primo aboard the *First Light*. "You've presented a primitive recording contributed by a lesser race. Surely you don't believe that worthy of a conclave."

Soft gasps whispered through the ranks of the Primo, and Celendra's eyes narrowed. Her voice was frosty when she spoke. "Do not mock me, Endari. I have irrefutable proof that the Void Wraith exist, and that proof has been made available to you. In addition, I offer testimony from eyewitnesses."

Dryker knew a cue when he saw one. He strode forward, walking onto the large, empty disk. All eyes were on him as he mounted the steps up to the raised dais, clearly intended for a speaker to address the conclave.

"The 'testimony' you offer comes from the same source as the recordings," Endari protested. He gazed down at the conclave, finding support from more than a few Primo. "Are we to listen to the theories and ramblings of lesser races now?"

"Let the human speak." The purple-skinned figure—the one called Kayton—finally spoke, his voice deep and gravelly. "We can judge for ourselves whether this is worthy of a conclave. I, for one, find the presented evidence disturbing. We cannot know if this new race is, in fact, the Void Wraith. Yet their technology is clearly derived from our own, and must therefore be investigated."

"Very well, if you both wish it we will proceed with this foolishness," Endari said, waving dismissively at Celendra. "Speak, human. Give us your limited understanding of galactic events."

"The Void Wraith are real, but I don't expect you to believe that," Dryker said, turning slowly atop the dais. He looked from Primo to Primo, a sea of emotionless faces. Tough crowd. "The data core I provided to Celendra contains something that should concern you far more: it shows an attack on one of your libraries, an attack perpetrated by your own people. I asked her to wait until today to show you that data, because it proves that at least some of your people are working with the Void Wraith."

"Lies," Endari barked. "Our people would never attack a library, not for any reason. Libraries are sacred. If one were attacked, it could only be by lesser races, and we would easily repel them."

"See for yourself," Celendra said, coldly.

She gestured, and the entire dome displayed a holographic image. It was a familiar scene, one that evoked painful memories. Three Primo carriers launching fighters to fire on the *Johnston*, then the *Johnston* speeding away toward the star. Behind them, more fighters attacked the Primo library. Plasma beams scored its pristine surface, and the damage worsened as the *Johnston* retreated. Then the library exploded in a wave of intense white light. The dome went translucent again.

"Why have you waited until now to show us this?" Kayton asked. He leaned toward Celendra, almost threateningly.

"Because of what it means," Celendra said. "Dryker is right. We have been infiltrated by the Void Wraith. It is possible that some of the people in this room are actively working to destroy our race."

14

SHIPWARMING PRESENT

Nolan circled warily, prowling the edge of the dueling circle as Fizgig did the same just a few feet away. The pair watched each other, each waiting for a weakness.

"Hey, Nolan, if you're through getting your ass kicked I brought you a present," Annie said, drawing Nolan's gaze.

It was a fatal error. In the split second Nolan's gaze was averted, Fizgig darted forward and rammed her plasma blade into his chest. His muscles spasmed in the by-now familiar pain of paralysis, and he flopped about for several agonizing seconds, clawing the deck as he waited for the pain to subside.

"You let Annie's arrival distract you. Such distractions are common in combat. They separate the warriors from the kits. Kits will chase whatever draws their attention," Fizgig said, offering Nolan a paw. He accepted it and she effortlessly heaved him to his feet. "You must be more than that. You must be a predator, fixed on your prey. If your focus is greater, then you will be ready to take advantage of *their* lapse in attention."

Like all of Fizgig's lessons, this one was practical and easy to understand. Nolan nodded, bending to pick up his towel as he walked over to the doorway. "Same time tomorrow?"

"Of course," Fizgig said, nodding. She leaned forward to lick her forearm, then glanced back at him. "You have impressed me, Nolan. You learn quickly. Pursue this with the same persistence you have pursued strategy, and you will become deadly."

Nolan gave her a grateful nod, then joined Annie in the hallway. She carried a large brown sack that bulged with a rectangular object. A trail of red and yellow wiring, long enough to brush the floor, hung from the bag.

"Is that what I think it is?" Nolan asked, toweling sweat from his face.

"Yep," Annie said cheerfully. "I figure Bock will get by without one for a few days, and none of the miners care. Coronas will pay for a replacement. I can have it installed on the bridge whenever you like, but if you want something quick and dirty all it needs is power. There are conduits all over the ship."

"Okay, let's get it installed then," Nolan said, starting for the bridge. He was quiet as they walked, considering Annie's actions. They were a little ruthless, but also pragmatic. They'd needed a quantum transmitter, so she'd acquired one.

Underhanded, but the longer Nolan played this game the more he realized principles could get you killed. Principles were the reason Admiral Kelley had died in his sleep. Yet if one gave up one's principles, what was left? It was a troubling line of thought.

He trotted up the last set of stairs, striding onto the

bridge. "Set it up on the far wall there; you can wire it to that access panel."

Nolan moved to the hastily-installed captain's chair, sitting stiffly on the sharply angular metal. It wasn't comfortable, but it beat standing for the entire shift. He watched as Annie worked quickly and efficiently. She had the access panel off and the wiring exposed within seconds. It didn't take much more than a minute for her to connect the red and yellow wires to the pulsing blue lines that powered their ship.

"The nice thing about these portable transmitters," Annie said, closing the access panel, "is that they have limiters built in. It will automatically regulate the flow of power it draws from the ship."

"That's it? You installed a quantum transmitter into an alien vessel, and all it took was two minutes of your time?" Nolan asked, raising an eyebrow.

"I'm pretty good with this stuff, but it's just not that hard," she said, shrugging. She pressed the green button on the front of the transmitter and it hummed to life. "The network strength is really weak. You can't check your messages in your bunk or anything, but at least we should be dialed in now."

Nolan got out his comm. It was already syncing, the tiny *QN* logo swirling across the screen. A moment later, his home screen began to populate, and he saw he'd missed several messages. He thumbed open the app, selecting a message.

Kathryn had requested a meeting for the following day.

"Annie, get the crew together. Looks like we're taking a trip to Mulholland Station," Nolan said, hitting the *Reply* button.

15

MULHOLLAND STATION

N olan was more than a little jittery as he entered Mulholland Station's food court. Hundreds of people flowed between tables, each carrying trays from one of the station's eleven restaurants. They were all different flavors and cuts of the same basic soy protein served in backwaters like this, but after three months in dead space they smelled heavenly.

"It's so weird being around this many people," he muttered under his breath, knowing Hannan would pick it up. She'd injected him with a sub-dermal transmitter just before they'd arrived. He couldn't hear his team, but they would know everything he knew, as soon as he knew it.

Nolan carried his tray to an empty table and sat down to wait. He glanced around him as he used the chopsticks to shovel noodles into his mouth as quickly as he could get them from the bowl to his face. God, he'd missed real food. As the noodles disappeared, his pace slowed, and he began to survey the crowd a little more carefully.

The guards lurking on the fringes of the crowd carried stun batons, but no firearms. That made sense. The superdense hull of a starship was designed to pass through a star. Small arms had no prayer of punching through them, no matter the caliber. But stations like Mulholland were built cheap, and since they were stationary the developers hadn't given them more than a thin steel membrane. Bullets were a real hazard here, which was why station security was so strict.

Nolan had no firearm, but he *did* have a plasma blade. He'd tucked the bracelet under the leather coat he'd borrowed from Annie. The coat was loose around the gut, but fit snugly around his arms and shoulders. The bracelet didn't even make a bulge in the arm, and what-ever scan the security guards had used hadn't seemed to pick it up.

"Nolan?" came a familiar voice from behind him. It cut through the din, drowning out everything else. He shifted in his seat to see Kathryn, just as she dropped into the chair across from him. She shot him a dazzling smile, but there was something...*off* about it. It didn't quite reach her eyes. Stress maybe?

Nolan wasn't really sure how he felt about seeing her. They'd never been a couple, not officially, but things had been headed that direction right before he'd been exiled to the 14th. She'd been wrapped up in that, though he didn't hold it against her. Admiral Mendez had likely strong-armed her just as he had Nolan. Either way, Kathryn had helped them a lot. It was only because of her that they'd even known about the Ghantan system.

"It's good to see you, Kathryn," Nolan said, smiling back. He meant it. It *was* good to see her, even if he couldn't stop looking over his shoulder.

"I know we could go on for a while with small talk, but we can do that when we're somewhere safer. Bring me up to speed," she said, lowering her voice. "Where have you been, and what the hell happened out there?"

Nolan considered the question for half a second before answering. Could he trust her? Could he trust anyone? Right now he needed her, and that made the decision for him. He'd trust her as far as necessary, but he wasn't taking any chances.

"The war with the Tigris is the most massive coverup of all time," he said, hunching over his noodles and leaning a little closer. "The Tigris were there to help us against the Void Wraith. We blew up a factory, and stopped a bomb we believe they intended for Theras Prime."

"Theras Prime?" she asked, cocking her head in surprise. The gesture was a little too practiced, a little too OFI.

That gave Nolan pause, because he'd received the same training. Kathryn's surprise was feigned. Did she already know about Theras Prime? If so, how had she known? Why hide it? Nolan thought quickly, not liking where his line of logic led. There's only one reason Kathryn would lie, one way she could have known. She'd been compromised.

How the hell was he going to disengage? If she was lying, had she brought friends? Or was he just being paranoid and misreading her emotions?

16

KATHRYN

Kathryn stretched out a hand, resting it gently on Nolan's for a moment. Then she leaned back, taking him in. He'd changed in the last few months, though it was difficult to put her finger on the *how* of it. He was more confident, certainly, but there was more to it than that. He moved differently.

"Yeah, Theras Prime," he said, after a pause. He busied himself with his noodles, scarfing them like a war refugee. Was he avoiding her gaze?

"Okay, so you dealt with this bomb," Kathryn said, picking her words carefully. He must not suspect the joining; her larva had been clear on that. "What happened after? Why have you been gone so long? And what ship are you on? The *Johnston* was presumed destroyed."

"One question at a time," Nolan said, his face unreadable. He was more guarded than he'd been when they'd last worked together. That was also new, and problematic. Earnest Nolan was much easier to read. "The bomb destroyed the star, and we had to fly to another one. It took a few months to reach another star with a Helios Gate, and we've been out of contact that entire time. My turn. What happened to you? Have you officially gone rogue? I notice you're still flying the *Sparhawk*."

"I'm officially AWOL," she said, glancing around to make sure they weren't being eavesdropped on. This part she'd been ready for. "Most of the admiralty has been infiltrated, I think. I couldn't risk sticking around, so I grabbed *Sparhawk* and ran." She took a sip of Nolan's soda, giving him a playful smile.

"And in the three months since?" Nolan asked, ignoring the theft. His expression remained impassive.

"My turn," she said, touching his hand again. "What ship are you on?"

"One of the Void Wraith harvesters. We commandeered it during the battle," Nolan said. He polished off the rest of his noodles, sighing as he set the bowl down. "Your turn. Catch me up on the last three months."

"I've been running from port to port. The war with the Tigris is heating up, so patrols along the fringes are next to nonexistent," Kathryn explained. "The only fleet defending the periphery is the 14th, and they're stretched pretty thin. I figured I'd be safe out here, and so far I'm right. My turn. What did you learn about the Void Wraith? Where do they come from?"

The question was casual, but she felt the quivering around her spine. The larva was *very* interested in Nolan's answer.

Nolan was silent for a long moment. Too long. *He knew.* She must have done something to betray her true loyalties. That scared the hell out of her, because she knew what the larva would make her do. Perhaps they could finish the exchange. She'd get what information she could, and they'd part ways. The masters hadn't demanded his death, and that part of her mind, the part grown by the larva, was silent.

"They've been here a long time," Nolan said. He glanced right, then left, and his tone was even lower when he continued, barely audible over the hum of the crowd. "The empire before the Primo dark ages wasn't the first. My crew is investigating the empire before that. We believe it predated the Void Wraith, because the Primo DNA from that time wasn't modified. Their DNA now? It's got markers all over it. Someone or something engineered changes in the Primo. That something shaped the Primo into the Void Wraith, and I think we're close to cracking who it might be."

Fire raced up Kathryn's spine. It grew, spreading along her nervous system, flooding her limbs. She recognized the fire, of course. It was the larva connecting to its distant parent. It only did that when it needed to seek council about something, and in this case Kathryn knew exactly what it was doing—what question it was asking.

"If we can get to a Primo library, I have someone on my crew who believes she can learn the origins of the Void Wraith," Nolan said.

The words had doomed him. Kathryn knew it instantly. She knew it before the fire receded, before the larva seized control of her nervous system. She could do nothing as her hand scythed out toward Nolan's throat. She knew he was dead, because Nolan wasn't a field agent. He'd never been trained to fight—only to think.

Kathryn's surprise was total when Nolan ducked to the right and batted her attack aside. He leapt backward, keeping the table between him. Even as the shock registered, she was vaulting the table, aiming a kick at his face. He snapped up a forearm, smoothly blocking the blow.

"Take him alive," Reid screamed from the crowd behind

her. She was aware of Delta moving toward her, and realized she might actually need his help to subdue Nolan.

17

RUN

Nolan was shocked when his hand shot up of its own accord, knocking Kathryn's blow aside. He was even more surprised when he fended off the next several blows, backpedaling to gain room. Kathryn was a trained OFI field agent, and had several years experience in hand-to-hand combat. Nolan had three months of Fizgig's tutelage.

Of course, Kathryn was nothing compared to Fizgig. Her speed wasn't as blinding, and she wasn't nearly as strong. She was, he realized, an opponent he might actually be evenly matched with. Especially if he used his plasma blade.

Then Nolan saw Delta, Doctor Reid's number one enforcer. Nolan and his crew had, he'd thought, rescued Delta during that long-ago attack on Coronas 6, and had turned him over to Admiral Mendez. Nolan realized several things in that instant. After he'd handed Delta to Mendez, Mendez had probably given him right back to Reid. Delta had been a prisoner in name only, and everything Nolan had thought he'd accomplished back on that station was a lie.

Nolan also realized that Kathryn was working with Delta, which meant she was working with Reid. There was only one way that could have happened. His suspicions were right. She'd been compromised by the Void Wraith.

Shit. Without a second thought Nolan turned and sprinted through the crowd, keeping as many people between himself and Delta as possible. He was aware of Kathryn pounding across the metal floor behind him, and he did his best to gain ground as he ducked past a startled family looking for a place to sit.

"I hope we've got a quick escape plan," Nolan panted into his comm. He knew Hannan and Annie were probably watching, but there wasn't much they'd be able to do to intervene directly. Not without firearms. Station security was already moving to intercept—whether him, or his pursuers, was hard to tell.

Nolan risked a glance over his shoulder, his bowels filling with ice water as he caught sight of Delta's face just half a dozen paces back. The enormous black man sprinted through the crowd, people dodging out of his path as he gained on Nolan. Delta's metallic arms had been painted a flat black, which somehow made them look even more lethal. Nolan vividly remembered being punched by one of those fists, and wasn't eager to repeat the experience.

He scanned the path ahead, looking for options. There weren't any. Taking the escalator would slow him down enough for Delta to catch up, but he had to be on the lower level to get to the airlock. Nolan skidded to a halt next to the railing overlooking the promenade. The station had two floors, and it was about a twenty-foot drop from here to the next level.

Nolan jumped, aware of Delta's fingers brushing his arm as he fell out of sight.

He rolled with the landing, just like Fizgig had showed him. A sharp pain shot through his right leg, but thankfully the adrenaline suppressed it. He rolled back to his feet and started sprinting for the far end of the station. Shoppers stopped to stare, but not at Nolan; they were looking behind him, and Nolan didn't have to turn around to know why. He heard a large crack, and knew it was the sound of Delta's heavy frame landing on the tile behind him.

Ahead, he spotted Annie, who was holding the outer airlock door open. Nolan poured on the speed, ignoring the pain in every step. He sprinted fast and low, rapidly reducing the distance to the airlock.

Out of the corner of his eye, he saw Delta closing on the right. Nolan swerved left, dropping into a slide that carried him under a table. He flipped back to his feet on the other side, going right back into a sprint. Delta had still gained on him, and was just a few feet back and to the left.

Nolan was positive he wasn't going to make it, but less than ten feet from the door Hannan popped out of cover behind a fake potted palm tree. She held a four-foot steel tube, and Nolan didn't want to know where she'd gotten it. Hannan wound up, swinging the tube with all her considerable strength. It caught Delta in the face, shattering his jaw and knocking him to the ground.

"Let's move," Hannan said, dropping the pipe. She moved to Nolan, wrapping an arm around him. "Lean on me. You're limping."

Nolan staggered the last few feet into the airlock, gasping pained breaths as Annie slammed the hatch behind them.

18

PRIMO CONCLAVE

Dryker wished he had a sidearm, though it would have been useless—nothing more than a security blanket, but one he'd have accepted gratefully. He stared around at the sea of hostile Primo faces, though, thankfully, their hostility was largely directed at each other. Celendra's words hung over them. They'd been infiltrated by the Void Wraith. It was a bitter pill to swallow, assuming they were willing to do that. He still remembered how he'd felt when he realized the admiralty was compromised.

"This accusation is unprecedented," Endari shouted, quieting the cacophony of the Primo down to a low murmur. "As such, it dramatically changes the importance of this conclave. If Celendra's charges are true, clearly steps must be taken. *If* they are true."

"Yes, *if*," Kayton said in a deep voice. His purple skin gleamed, and Dryker guessed he was the youngest of the Primo leaders. Kayton stared hard at Celendra. "Do you have any evidence beyond a simple holorecording? Any proof of wrongdoing, or a list of those you feel may be infected?"

Celendra gave a pained look, then shook her head wordlessly.

"So," Endari said, drawing out the word. "You have no real evidence, then, just supposition. Supposition that will turn our race against itself, ensuring that ship battles ship, until we rejoin the cosmic dust that gave birth to us all."

"I understand that this is difficult to accept," Celendra countered, looking to the gathered Primo for support. Dryker couldn't read their faces very well, but he didn't think she was finding that support. "And I know that, at least right now, all evidence is circumstantial. But hear my words before you cast judgement. We all know that our race rose from the ashes of some great cataclysm. Something so heinous that it cast us down into the dark ages, centuries where we lost culture, and civilization itself was nearly lost.

"Is it really so great a stretch to assume that this cataclysm was caused by the Void Wraith? Or that they might, even now, be influencing some among our number? How else would you explain the attack on the library?" Celendra asked. There were murmurs of agreement now. "We can all see that the attack took place, and while we cannot identify the ships involved, they *are* Primo. How would you explain this attack?"

A flash caught Dryker's attention. It came from outside the transparent dome above them, and as he looked up he saw another flash. And another. The flashes were blue, the familiar blue of Void Wraith weaponry. Dozens of Void Wraith harvesters were de-cloaking, the V-shaped vessels delivering catastrophic damage to the unprepared Primo fleet.

"We're under attack," Dryker boomed in his best drill sergeant voice. "The Void Wraith are tearing this fleet apart."

A human crowd would have panicked, probably scattering into a hundred different directions. The Primo were alien, and their reaction reflected it. They froze, each going silent and staring up at the three figures hovering above them.

"We must return to our ships!" Kayton roared. "Quickly, or this battle is lost."

"This battle is already lost," Celendra said, staring sadly up. "We must send out the word to retreat. Now, while something of our people still survives."

"Kayton is right," Endari said, straightening on his throne. He peered down at the Primo. "We must return to our ships. Back to your shuttles, ready yourselves for battle."

Dryker turned to look at Khar, who shrugged helplessly. He could feel the frustration radiating off the cat, and shared it. The Primo were being overwhelmed, and they needed decisive leadership—leadership they clearly lacked.

"Listen up!" Dryker shouted. Primo all around him froze again, turning to look at him. "If you return to your ships, you are dooming your people. Celendra is right. Our one chance is to send a broadcast to all vessels, right now. Tell them to flee for the Helios Gate. Do it now, or your entire race will be harvested by this time tomorrow. Theras is already gone. Look around you."

That had an effect. The Primo looked to their leaders. All three were staring at Dryker, but it was Kayton who spoke. "Very well. The human echoes Celendra, and it rings of sense. Broadcast a signal to all vessels. Tell them to flee. Celendra, my family begs your hospitality until we can return to our own vessel."

"Granted," Celendra said, turning to Endari. "What of you? Will you stay and live, or extinguish the light of our people here and now?"

Endari looked trapped, glancing down at his people, then back up to Celendra. "Very well, we shall see if your rash decision has merit. My family will stay as well. Order the fleet to withdraw."

Celendra waved a hand, and a blue holographic panel appeared before her. She tapped buttons with blinding speed, and a moment later many of the Primo vessels turned to the sun. The *First Light* began to accelerate, and the perspective of the battle changed.

Dryker realized not every ship was heading for the sun. Roughly a third had stayed, and were helping the Void Wraith finish off Primo vessels too slow to reach the Helios Gate.

19

RECOVERY

"It's not broken," Lena said, rolling Nolan's ankle in a slow circle. It hurt, but not nearly as badly as he'd feared it would. "Stay off it as much as you can for a few days, and you'll be fine." She rose from her crouch, dusting off her hands on her clothing.

"Thanks, Lena. I'll do that as much as I can." Nolan knew the words were mechanical, but his mind was still back on Mulholland Station. Kathryn was working with Delta. Maybe they'd implanted her with a control chip, or maybe they'd used something else. The cause didn't really matter. What did was the fact that their one potential ally had been turned. Dryker was either dead or missing. It was a lot to take in.

Hannan and Izzy filed into the makeshift conference room, sliding into seats next to Fizgig. Nolan waited for them to be seated before speaking. "I'm going to be brutally honest. Kathryn has clearly been converted, which leaves us without any safe human contacts. After what happened back there we have no allies."

"What *did* happen? You two were talking, and then she

took a swing," Hannan said, pulling out her plasma pistol and a rag.

"Good question," Nolan said, thinking back to the moments preceding the fight. "We were talking about Primo libraries, and about the first Primo empire. Then I mentioned the Void Wraith origins."

"Interesting," Fizgig said, her tail swishing lazily. "That fact may be coincidence, but I do not think so."

"The Void Wraith appear to be trying to stop the dissemination of any information about the Primo's past," Lena said, her golden ears twitching.

"I'd agree. The question is *why*. What don't they want us finding out? You don't go to these lengths to hide something, unless it coming to light would be catastrophic," Nolan asked. "Lena, you're our best hope of answering that question. Do you have any theories?"

Lena stood and began pacing. She completed several circuits before speaking. "There must be something in the Primo archives that relates to the earlier incarnations of their empires, perhaps something about the genetic modifications the Void Wraith made. Something that would give us an advantage, or help us fight them."

"Perhaps..." Izzy said, softly. Her eyes widened when everyone looked at her.

"Did you have a thought, sister?" Lena asked, placing an encouraging paw on Izzy's shoulder.

Izzy peered around, wide-eyed, then cleared her throat.

"If we find out who the Void Wraith are, then we might learn about who made them. I don't believe the Void Wraith are merely shock troops. I think they are also a way to protect the identity of their creators. They used them to subdue the Primo without ever revealing their identity, just as they're doing now. Whoever made the Void Wraith is probably controlling both humans and Tigris, and they may fear that we might be able to break that control," Izzy said, hesitantly. "Perhaps they fear us learning their true identity. If we can expose them, perhaps we can root out the infiltrators."

"It's as good a theory as any. Izzy, see if you can help Lena puzzle some of this out," Nolan said, rising from the conference table. "Now we just need to find a library and convince the Primo to let us dock. Whatever the answer is, it will be found there. Ship, plot a course to the closest library and get us underway."

20

BLOW THEM UP

Delta spooned warm paste into his mouth, watching out of the corner of his eye as Reid and Kathryn argued. They tended to ignore him entirely during such outbursts, which were becoming increasingly more common as Reid's health deteriorated. The fact that Nolan had escaped had seemed to unhinge the pasty man, and his gaze was wild and unsteady now.

"The Eye is concerned," Reid said, pointing shakily at Kathryn. "I know you feel it. You must. The burning, your whole body on fire. The Eye demands action."

"I feel it," Kathryn said, her face drawn and pale. "But you can't let it control you, Reid. Now, more than ever, we need our composure. We need to stop Nolan, and doing that is going to be more difficult than either of us anticipated. Before we go any further, we need to inform my father, so he can deploy vessels to help hunt Nolan down."

Kathryn didn't wait for a response, instead activating the table's holodisplay. It showed the standard Quantum connecting icon, then resolved into Admiral Mendez's face. Despite the late hour, the bearded man was seated at his desk. Delta wondered if the admiral still slept, or if their parasites removed the need.

"Kathryn? Do you have something to report?" Mendez asked. He glanced briefly at Reid, eyes widening.

"Nolan escaped," Kathryn said, straightening as if bracing for a blow. "He's aboard a harvester, but seemed genuinely out of the loop. I think he's sincere about just having returned."

"I'm not surprised. I warned you, Reid," Mendez said, sighing.

Reid ignored him, muttering into his hands and rocking back and forth.

Mendez looked back to Kathryn. He reached into his desk drawer, removing a cigar. The remains of several sat in the usually pristine ashtray. "In a harvester, you say? That will make it impossible to track him. How much did he learn from the encounter?"

"Too much," Kathryn said, sighing. Delta eyed her, privately pleased at the situation. Nolan was a good soldier, trying his best to stop an unstoppable threat. Delta might not be able to help, but he could admire what the man was doing. "He's stumbled onto information about the original Primo. He knows they existed, and that something converted them into the Void Wraith."

"Does he know anything about the Birthplace?" Mendez demanded, straightening. Kathryn clearly had his full attention now.

"I don't know," Kathryn admitted. "We didn't have him there long enough to find out. You can see the predicament we're in. We have to find Nolan, but I don't know how."

"Mmmm," Mendez said, resting his chin on his fingers. "There's nothing we can do to accurately track him, so we need an alternative plan. If he wants to learn about the Birthplace there's only one place he can do that."

"A Primo library," Kathryn said. She shifted uncomfortably. "How do we find out which one he's going to go to?"

"We don't," Mendez said, giving a grim smile. "We wipe them all out, as quickly as possible. As long as they exist, they're a danger. The surviving Primo are in no condition to protect them, so we'll never have a better opportunity. I'll order harvesters to deal with as many libraries as possible."

"Doctor Reid, are you okay with that decision?" Kathryn asked, finally turning her attention back to the pasty doctor.

Delta saw her shrink back from the man as he turned to face her.

"The Eye has demanded my presence," Reid said, in a small voice. He pushed his glasses up on his nose, peering at them through the grime. "We will go to meet it, while Mendez destroys these libraries. Leave none standing."

21

THINK LIKE A HUMAN

Dryker stared out the window at the few Primo ships that had escaped the massacre at Theras Prime. There were only six, and two of those six were leaking a dangerous amount of blue plasma from huge gashes in their hulls. At least one was doomed, and the other might not be able to handle another passage through a star. They were in bad shape.

"We could try to escape," Khar rumbled. He moved to stand next to Dryker. "The *Claw of Tigrana* can fly. Juliard has assisted my warriors in repairing her over the last few months. She isn't in perfect fighting shape, but we could reach Leonis Pride. Or perhaps your government."

"I doubt the Primo would let us get far if we tried to slip away," Dryker said, stroking his beard as he considered. He'd let it go at some point in the last month, and it had begun to itch as it got longer. "Their ego is on the line. No, I think a different tack is in order. Juliard, you up for a little walk?"

"Sir?" the blonde lieutenant asked, blinking up at him.

"We're going to crash the Primo council meeting,"

Dryker said, smiling grimly. He strode to the doorway, pausing long enough to make sure both were following. He had no idea how the Primo would react, but presenting a united front was the best way to make sure they took him seriously.

He plunged ahead, walking down wide corridors that wound toward the heart of the ship. They arrived at the same chamber where the conclave had taken place, but this time the meeting was much smaller. Maybe a dozen Primo stood watching, while the three principle players floated on the thrones above.

Dryker wasn't sure how their leadership worked, but he thought he was starting to puzzle it out. Each vessel had a navigator, and that navigator served as a spokesperson for the crew. They weren't captains in the traditional sense, as they appeared to need the support of their crew. Perhaps it was an elected position. Regardless, the key to changing their decision lay in getting them to worry what their crews might think.

"I believe we might find aid in the Elonias system," Kayton was saying. "We might be able to link up with the other survivors, which would make us a considerable force —perhaps the largest remaining."

Dryker strode boldly into the room, walking onto the central dais. Everyone turned to look at him, and the purple-skinned Primo's eyes narrowed. Dryker didn't care.

"You had your *entire fleet* at Theras. How did that work out for you?" Dryker said, gesturing at the dome above. The Primo looked up just in time to see a fresh jet of blue plasma leak from the side of one of the doomed vessels.

"Have you come to mock us, or do you present a better plan, human?" Endari said, leaning forward to scowl down at Dryker.

"Yes, I do have a better plan," Dryker said, folding his arms and scowling back. "Make an alliance with the Tigris, and with humanity. Work together to stop the Void Wraith. If you try to do this on your own, you're doomed. That's exactly what the Void Wraith want: they want the scattered remnants of your fleet to gather in one place, because it will make it easy to wipe you out."

"Your species are at war," Endari retorted, the words heavy with derision. "They cannot stop their own squabble. How will they help us?"

"Are you blind?" Dryker snapped. He didn't try to reign in his anger, instead using it to fuel his next words. "A third of your fleet worked *with* the Void Wraith. I've been telling you for months that they've infiltrated *all* of our races. The human-Tigris conflict is a product of their intervention. If you release Khar to go to his people, and me to go to mine, perhaps we can stop this conflict and get our races to work together."

Murmuring rustled through the assembled Primo. Dryker knew it was unlikely they'd listen, but it was all he had.

"Mighty Primo," Khar said, stepping up next to Dryker. His tail swished behind him, and his ears were as erect as Dryker had ever seen. "I would add the weight of my own words to my human friend's. I say *friend*, because we are indeed friends—brothers in this fight against an enemy that would seek to reduce us all to unthinking slaves. My people need me. Dryker's people need him. We must be allowed to help them overcome this threat, not just for our own sakes, but for yours. We can bring you allies in this fight, allies you desperately need."

"Releasing them runs the risk of exposing us," Kayton said, though there was no heat to the words this time. He looked to Celendra. "What say you? This is your vessel, and they your guests."

"Are you mad?" Endari interrupted. His throne drifted closer to the others, and Dryker had to strain to hear his next words. "If we release them, we alert the Void Wraith agents among both the humans and the Tigris that our vessels survived. They must not be released."

"I am not mad, but I have been blind," Celendra replied, her loud, clear voice echoing through the room. "Our fleet is in ruins, our people lost and divided. Before that happened, before we were attacked by the Void Wraith, did those we call lesser not tell us it would occur? Dryker is a great leader among his people, a canny warrior. Yet we did not heed his advice, and thousands of our people paid the price. For the first time in our history, our extinction has become a possibility."

"Then you'd have us release them?" Kayton said, raising a pensive hand to cup his own chin.

"No," Celendra said, looking down at Dryker with those unreadable red eyes. "I would have us place our forces under their command. The spies among the Primo expect us to think like Primo. If we are to have a chance at survival, we cannot be predictable. Allowing a human to craft our battle strategy is something they will never expect."

The room was completely still, the only movement Khar's swishing tail.

"You are Mighty Dryker," Khar said, purring loudly. "Even the Primo recognize it."

The Primo were in an uproar, one that three leaders seemed unable to quell. Celendra called for order several times before the crowd finally subsided enough for her to speak.

"As this is my vessel, I can give you power over the military decisions I make," she said, then turned to the purple-skinned Primo. "Kayton, what say you? Will you give your own people into his charge as well, for the duration of the war?"

"This is a hasty decision," Kayton said, his eyes flaring brightly for a moment. "Yet it is one I suspect you ruminated on before the attack. How long have you been planning this?"

"I've seen the need for different thinking for some time," Celendra said. "The lesser races are more prolific than we. They advance much more quickly. They are bold, and inquisitive. We are neither. If we wish to survive, we need their help."

Dryker knew her words were anathema to most hearing them. The Primo prided themselves on being the oldest and best race. They were more intelligent and more advanced than anyone else, and hearing one of their leaders admit they needed the lesser races...well, that had to be a bitter pill to swallow.

"You were right to do so," Kayton said, straightening to his full height. He stared imperiously down at his people, then turned to Dryker and Khar. "Giving charge of my vessel to a human may be the height of folly, but I see little choice. Let us place our fate in the hands of the lesser races, and hope that they prove worthy of the trust."

"I will not be a party to this," Endari hissed, his tiny mouth turning down into a steep frown. His throne began drifting lower. "My family and I will depart, and make our own way."

The hall fell silent as Endari rose shakily from his throne. A guard approached, offering Endari a walking staff. The grey-skinned Primo snatched it from the guard, waddling toward a corridor. His followers, nearly a fifth of the Primo in the room, departed. Their numbers had been small to begin with, and this reduced them further.

"What would you have us do, Captain Dryker?" Celendra's clear voice rang out again.

"First, we've got to find a way to stop the war between humanity and the Tigris. Do you have access to our Quantum Network?" Dryker asked. The admiralty had long suspected the Primo could infiltrate their network, but had never confirmed it.

"We do. I will have a device brought to your quarters. Have you further orders?" Celendra asked.

"Send as many techs as you can spare to assist Khar. The *Claw of Tigrana* will need your help in restoring her," Dryker said, nodding at Khar.

"Done. We will see that he has all he needs," Celendra said.

Dryker smiled for the first time in a long while. He could finally communicate with the outside world, and that meant maybe—just maybe—he could get in contact with Nolan.

22

CONNECTING

"Captain." Ship's pleasant voice interrupted Nolan, and he looked up from the tactical simulation he'd created on the holomap. It showed a group of harvesters engaging a human fleet. It wasn't going well for the humans, but Nolan had seen at least a few tactics that might improve their odds.

"What is it, Ship?" Nolan asked.

"You asked to be notified if you received a priority message from a specific list of personages. You have just received a message from a Captain Dryker. It's marked priority. Shall I read it to you?"

"Yes," Nolan said, rising from the simulation and hurrying from the room. If he wanted to reply he'd need to be on the bridge, near the transmitter.

"Need to meet, soonest," Ship cheerfully delivered. "All communications unsafe."

Nolan leapt to his feet. He broke into a full run, whooping as he ran through the hall. He sucked in a deep breath, yelling loud enough to carry. "Dryker made contact. All hands to the bridge."

He didn't wait for the others to show up, dropping into a chair next to the blocky transmitter, whipping out his comm, and bringing up the message.

Time and Place, he wrote. Then he hit *Send*.

Less than three seconds later, his screen flickered, and a request for a video feed popped up. Nolan was doubly surprised. There should have been no way for Dryker to have responded to the message that quickly.

Nolan pressed the video icon, and the screen showed a blue Primo face. It was dominated by flat, red eyes, which blinked slowly at him. "Commander Nolan?"

"Yes," Nolan said hesitantly. "That's me. Where's Dryker?"

The Primo turned from the screen and called over his shoulder. "I have him on the line, Captain Dryker."

The view shifted, and Nolan found himself staring at Dryker. The old man wore a huge grin. "You survived. I wasn't sure. Well done, Commander."

"It's Captain now—well, acting Captain anyway," Nolan said, smiling back.

The others were making their way onto the bridge. Hannan and Edwards were the first to arrive.

"Is that the captain—uh, I mean, Captain Dryker?" the cyborg said, settling into a crouch behind Nolan. His head still occasionally drew lines of sparks from the ceiling, but he was getting better at hunching as he walked.

"What the hell is that?" Dryker asked.

Nolan glanced up, and realized Dryker was looking at Edwards.

"That's Private Edwards, sir," Nolan replied. "We have a lot to catch up on."

"Clearly we do. Let's keep this short. We need to meet. Can you make best speed to the Enduria system?" It wasn't really a question. Nolan heard the order, but for the first time he didn't blindly obey. Nolan would do what Dryker asked, but because it was the right thing...not because he was following orders. The distinction was subtle, but powerful.

"We'll do that," Nolan replied, nodding. "See you in a few hours."

23

ARRIVALS

"Captain, we are clearing the sun's corona," Ship said, rousing Nolan from his data pad.

"Activate holographic display," Nolan said, rising from the stiff metal chair. He stretched, watching as the space before the wall filled with color and light. It resolved into a star field, but Nolan noticed something missing immediately. "Ship, where is the Primo library?"

"There is a debris field matching known Primo construction," Ship supplied. The holographic display zoomed in, showing hunks of floating metal rotating slowly. "It is likely the library has been destroyed. However, I am picking up a number of vessels in system."

"Show me," Nolan ordered.

Hannan and Izzy strode onto the bridge, chatting in low tones. They quieted when they saw Nolan, and he ignored them. Annie filed in a moment later, still brushing her teeth.

The holomap displayed a cluster of capital ships. Six Primo carriers, and one much smaller Tigris warship. "Ship, can you get me an ident on that Tigris vessel?"

"The ship is registered as the *Claw of Tigrana*," Ship supplied.

"The *Claw* survives?" Izzy said, blinking. Then she gave a very toothy grin, and turned to Hannan. "Mighty Fizgig must be told. Mighty Nolan, your permission to fetch her?"

"Granted," Nolan said, though he didn't see the need to grant her permission.

Izzy sprinted from the bridge, her tail held high behind her.

"Captain, we're being hailed by one of the Primo vessels," Ship said, a little more urgently.

"On screen," Nolan said, mostly out of habit. The harvester didn't have a screen, per se.

The hologram resolved into an unfamiliar room, all blue metal and elaborately decorated walls. A cluster of Primo stood in the background, but it was the figure in the foreground that drew Nolan's attention. He looked a little older, and more tired than Nolan had remembered, but he was alive.

"Hello, Captain Dryker," Nolan said, giving a warm smile. He wished the man were close enough to hug.

"Hello, Captain Nolan," Dryker replied, his leathery face splitting into a grin. "It's damned good to see you alive. Is that Hannan in the background there?"

"Hello, sir," Hannan called, giving a lazy salute.

"What say we meet face-to-face?" Dryker asked. "We have a lot to catch up on."

"Agreed," Nolan said, nodding. "We'll dock with you. Fizgig, Hannan, and I will be coming over."

"Great, see you shortly. Dryker out."

"Annie," Nolan said, turning to smile at her. "How do you feel about shuttling us over to that carrier?"

24

SHUTTLE

The ramp squealed loudly as it closed behind them. Nolan looked around the cargo hold of the *Tibs*, but there was no way he was going to be able to find a place to sit. Junk covered every surface, from half-repaired holorecorders to discarded food containers. It looked like Annie probably lived in her pilot's chair, as Nolan didn't see any place for her to bed down.

He picked his way through the junk, hiding a smile as he passed Lena. She'd plastered herself against a corner, staring at the shuttle in horror. To someone of Lena's upbringing, the lack of order here was probably physically painful. Neither Izzy nor Fizgig seemed perturbed by any of it. Fizgig stood stoically near the cockpit, and Izzy was a half-pace behind, trying to mimic Fizgig's stance.

"Best secure yourselves," Annie called over her shoulder, flicking a couple switches then seizing the yoke. She guided the shuttle off the deck with a shudder, and it rose shakily toward the wide bay door.

An electric tingle passed over Nolan's skin as they passed

through the harvester's protective membrane, and into open space. Annie guided the shuttle down and away, circling wide as they approached the group of Primo carriers. It was the first time Nolan had been this close to their vessels, and he leaned forward, drinking in every detail.

"Look at the size of those things," Hannan breathed.

"They're works of art," Fizgig said, giving an approving purr. "The Primo understand how to produce a truly formidable weapon of war."

"Not formidable enough to keep from getting their tails kicked, from the look of it," Nolan said, pointing at the furthest carrier. "Look at the plasma leaking from that one. The rest of them have taken battle damage as well. They've been through combat, and whoever they fought gave them one hell of a run for their money."

"Sir?" Hannan asked, turning the co-pilot's chair to face Nolan. "Did you happen to spot Mills with Captain Dryker? I didn't hear anything about him in Ghantan. I just wanted to know he was all right."

"I didn't," Nolan said, a spike of guilt shooting through his gut. He hadn't even thought about Mills, or about most of the *Johnston's* crew. Granted, he'd only been assigned to her for a few weeks before she was destroyed, but he still should have shown a bit more compassion. He put a hand on Hannan's shoulder. "I hope he's all right. If anyone could have gotten him out, it's Dryker."

"Holy crap on a stick," Annie said, drawing Nolan's attention back to the screen. They were close to the carrier where they'd been told to dock, and Annie had come around to one of the docking bays. Inside, they could see row after row of fighter drones. Each was larger than the *Tibs*, bristling with plasma cannons. "I really don't want to see whatever tangled with these guys and won."

Annie guided the shuttle into the bay, and Nolan clutched at the wall as they lurched to a halt on the deck.

25

COMPARING NOTES

Nolan was a bit surprised by the reception when he entered the Primo vessel. Twenty Primo stood at attention, each holding one of their ancestral war staffs. They offered a salute as he, Hannan, Lena, Izzy, and Fizgig filed past them.

"I don't know how the old man pulled it off, but he's got the Primo bowing and scraping," Hannan said, giving Nolan a sly grin. "You're getting better at this command stuff, but the old man is still the master."

"That he is," Nolan said, allowing another smile. The stresses of the past few days wore heavily on him, but he reminded himself there had been victories too. They'd stopped the Void Wraith in the Ghantan system, and they'd find a way to stop them again.

Their delegation was led into the most massive chamber Nolan had ever seen aboard a starship. He wasn't positive, but odds were good the *Sparhawk* could have fit into this chamber, with room to spare.

"Welcome, Captain Nolan," a clear voice rang out, echoing through the chamber. Nolan looked up to see a figure floating above, sitting atop a golden throne. She was a Primo, with light blue skin, dressed more elaborately than any of the others they'd seen so far. "I am Celendra, the Voice of the *First Light*. Welcome to my vessel."

"Thank you for allowing us to board," Nolan said, giving a stiff salute. He wasn't sure what the decorum was for boarding a Primo vessel, so he stuck to what he knew.

The Primo in the crowd behind Celendra seemed to appreciate the gesture, and Celendra gave an approving smile. "Please, be seated."

She gestured at a set of thrones very much like the one she sat in. One of those thrones was already occupied, and as Nolan approached, Dryker rose to greet him. Nolan reached out for a handshake, but the old man swept him into a hug.

"I'd feared the worst. It's good to see you, Nolan," Dryker said, giving him a tight squeeze, then releasing him. "Hello, Fizgig, I'm pleased to see you survived."

Fizgig and Izzy had moved to greet a male Tigris. It took Nolan a moment to recognize the Tigris as Khar. His face bore several new scars, but his fangs and claws were just as intimidating as ever. He wore a massive smile, his tail swishing back and forth behind him.

"Dryker," Fizgig said, turning from Khar and moving to stand next to Dryker and Nolan. "I am pleased to see you survived. Your new allies are...impressive."

"Yes, they are. Thanks to them, we were even able to save your ship," Dryker said, offering his hand to Fizgig.

"The *Claw* is my ship no longer," Fizgig said, accepting the captain's hand. "It rightfully belongs to Mighty Khar."

"For the moment. Challenge, and I will yield, Mighty Fizgig," Khar rumbled, swaggering his way over to them. He clapped Nolan hard on the shoulder, giving him a rather intimidating smile. "It is good to see you, Nolan. You have accomplished much since we battled the Void Wraith on the bridge of the *Johnston*."

"Captain?" Hannan asked quietly, stepping up to Dryker. Her eyes shone, and Nolan could tell she was struggling to get the words out. "Sir, did any of the crew survive? I don't see Mills."

Dryker's shoulders slumped, and for a moment he seemed to age decades. Then he straightened, resolve reentering his gaze. "I'm sorry, Hannan. Mills died getting us off the *Johnston*. He died the same way he lived, a Marine doing his duty."

Dryker reached into his pocket, withdrawing a clump of dog tags. The sheer number made Nolan wince. Dryker fished out a specific one, then handed it to Hannan. She took it wordlessly, giving Dryker a nod that somehow conveyed the depth of emotion she labored under. Then she turned and headed off the dais to stand near Annie.

"Apologies," Celendra's voice interrupted. All eyes rose to to the Primo. "My species prides itself on taking deliberate, slow action. Yet Dryker is teaching us the value of haste. Might we begin? There is much to discuss."

"Of course," Nolan said, taking a seat on one of the thrones. The others did the same.

Nolan inspected the device, noting a small array of buttons on the right arm of the throne. He couldn't read Primo sigils, but the icons seemed simple enough. He tapped the one on the top, and unsurprisingly the chair began to rise. Dryker's rose next, then Fizgig's. Within moments all of them hovered in the air near Celendra.

Below them milled something close to a hundred Primo, more than Nolan had ever seen in one place. He glanced up at Celendra, waiting for her to begin.

"We've gathered to discuss a course of action," Celendra called, her gaze sweeping the assembled Primo. "The Void Wraith have infiltrated our ranks. Even now, there could be spies among us. No race is safe, and it seems clear that the Void Wraith seek to wipe us out. Their motives remain unclear."

"Pardon, Celendra," Nolan interrupted. He waited for her to acknowledge him with a nod before speaking. "I can shed some light on their motives. The troops they use are created using our own kidnapped citizens. Judicators—their line troops—have the nervous system and brain of humans, Tigris, and Primo. They are, quite literally, turning our people against us. Their aim seems to be building a massive army, though the purpose of that army is unclear. We have evidence that this isn't the first, or even the second time that they've invaded the Milky Way. They show up on some sort of timetable, harvest our galaxy, and then leave us to rebuild."

Whispers rippled through the room, and Celendra looked visibly distressed. "That is troubling news, though the fact that you've puzzled out some of their motives is encouraging, at least. What else can you tell us of these Void Wraith?"

"We have detailed schematics of their weaponry, vessels, and line troops," Nolan explained. "Their technology is too similar to your own for it to be coincidence. The Void Wraith use technology that Lena guesses was pioneered during the first of three Primo empires."

Outraged shouts came from the crowd, most coming from older Primo. Celendra raised a hand, and most fell silent. There were still grumbles. Nolan saw Fizgig shifting back and forth on her throne, mouth turned down into a feline scowl. He'd seen that before, and knew her patience was wearing thin. At least her outburst, if it came, wouldn't be directed at him this time.

"Three?" Celendra said, looking deeply troubled. "I do not wish to doubt you, Captain, but this flies in the face of tens of thousands of years of history. Do you have proof you can submit? My people will demand it."

"I'll have that proof forwarded to you as soon as I return to my vessel," Nolan said, nodding. "It isn't conclusive, but there's enough to show that earlier empires did exist."

Fizgig leaned forward in her chair, drawing Nolan's attention. *Here it comes.*

"The motives of the Void Wraith are irrelevant, as is the history of your race," Fizgig boomed, drawing all eyes. She stared hard at Celendra. "A war rages between my people and the humans, a war based on a lie. Our priority is ending that war. We must convince both sides to lay down arms, and to unite against the Void Wraith. Every moment we spend debating minutiae, they draw the noose tighter around our necks."

26

DECISIONS

Fizgig was not pleased. It was all well and good that Dryker lived, and made allies of these Primo. Yet it changed nothing. Her people were hurling themselves into combat, dying while killing those who should be allies. It was maddening, especially because she was trapped here, unable to intervene.

She glared at Celendra, daring the Primo to take issue with her words.

Celendra blinked twice, then spoke. "I sometimes forget that Tigris are even more blunt than humans. You are not wrong; the issue of the war between your peoples must be addressed. Yet our own interest in this matter—"

"Your own interest?" Fizgig interrupted, leaning forward on the throne. She stared hard at the alien, nose twitching at the woman's odd scent. "It is exactly that kind of language that has made it so easy for the Void Wraith to infiltrate our ranks. If we are to survive, we must work for the benefit of everyone. We no longer have the luxury of our own self-interests."

"Fizgig is right," Nolan called, his deeper voice echoing from the chamber's high walls.

Fizgig fell silent, watching the kit appraisingly. He'd learned much under her tutelage, yet he was only human.

"Look around you," he continued. "That debris field is all that's left of a library that's been in this system for twenty-five millennia. We're losing this war so badly that we're not even fighting the real enemy. If we want to have any prayer of survival, then we must examine the situation tactically—not as separate races, but as a united coalition. That makes the war between humanity and the Tigris the most pressing issue. However, that doesn't mean we shouldn't explore other matters. Learning about our enemy is nearly as critical as stopping the war."

The human relaxed on his throne, watching Celendra. Fizgig continued to study him, waiting to see how the Primo would react. She knew nothing about their species, and the best way to learn about a foe was to watch, quietly. They'd reveal a weakness, and then, if circumstances dictated that they be eliminated, it was a simple matter to do so.

"If my people were to join a coalition, it would take months to set it up," Celendra said, giving a regretful sigh. "That simply isn't possible. I am the Voice and can speak for my vessel, at least. What would you have us do? I do not know the best way to proceed."

"First, you need a military leader," Fizgig said, without hesitation. "Strength flows from leadership. Without a strong leader, we are doomed."

"And who would you nominate for this position?" Celendra asked, cautiously.

"Mighty Fizgig!" Khar roared, raising his arms in an attempt to get others to take up the cry. Izzy did, but both fell quiet at a gesture from Fizgig.

"You introduced Dryker as a captain, did you not?" Fizgig asked, staring unblinkingly at the Primo.

"I did," Celendra answered, cocking her head to the side. "I do not understand the significance of the question."

"What is Dryker the captain of? He has no ship, unless you're telling me he's the captain of this vessel," Fizgig asked, her tail beginning to swish. She enjoyed baiting others, especially the Primo. They styled themselves superior, and it pleased her to educate this one.

"He is not the captain of the *First Light*. We do not have... captains. A Voice is merely a conduit for the will of the people," Celendra explained, clearly confused.

"Yet you are following the commands of Dryker, are you not?" Fizgig asked, another leading question.

"We are. Fizgig, I must admit that your questions are... irksome. What does any of this have to do with our current circumstances?" Celendra said. Fizgig wouldn't have called her angry, exactly. But she was clearly getting there. Good. Let her feel a tenth of the rage boiling in Fizgig.

"Among the humans, they have a rank that describes the position you've assigned Dryker," Fizgig said, purring softly.

"She wants to promote me to Admiral," Dryker called, eyeing Fizgig reproachfully. "Stop toying with her, Fizgig. We need their cooperation, and antagonizing them only makes the situation worse."

"I...see," Celendra said, regaining a measure of her composure. "Very well, we will promote Dryker to Admiral, if this title will help in some way."

"It isn't the title," Fizgig said, eyes narrowing to slits. "It is the authority that goes with it. Dryker must be freed to deal with the war as he sees fit."

"And what will you be doing during all this? You're just as qualified to run the fleet. More so, I think," Dryker said.

Fizgig met his gaze. He was one of the few humans she considered a true equal. One of the few among any species, truth be told. "There is only one way the Tigris would have gone to war as we did," she said, growling low in her throat. "Admiral Mow must have lied to them. If they believed that humans had wiped out our fleet, they'd have raced to war. That means that Admiral Mow has almost certainly been corrupted by these Void Wraith. I intend to challenge him for leadership."

"You'll need a vessel to do that, Mighty Fizgig," Khar pointed out, nodding deferentially as he spoke. "The *Claw of Tigrana* still fights. We can get you to Mow."

"And what of us, Admiral Dryker? What would you have us do?" Celendra asked.

Dryker was silent for a long time, gaining another pawful of respect. He took his time answering, even under the weight of the conclave's attention. "Fizgig can deal with her people. I need to deal with mine. There's every likelihood that the majority of the admiralty is now corrupt, but we can still gain support with the 14th fleet. We'll start there."

"Before we make these decisions, there's a lot we need to share about the Void Wraith origins," Nolan said. He hesitated, but only for a moment. Fizgig watched as his mind worked, piecing together what she'd already realized. "You already considered that, didn't you?"

"I did," Dryker said, nodding. "The sad fact is that we don't know who we can trust. We will discuss your findings in private, and I'll make a decision about how to proceed."

"Will my people be represented in this meeting?" Celendra asked, leaning forward to study Dryker intently. A sheen of milky sweat had broken out on her forehead, the first Fizgig had ever seen on a Primo.

"If you'd like to be represented," Dryker said, "we'll hold the meeting on the *Claw of Tigrana*."

Fizgig was pleased. She'd maneuvered Dryker into a role she detested, freeing her to tear out Mow's throat.

27

FEEDING THE EYE

"You're certain of these coordinates?" Delta asked, scanning the data pad. He looked up at Doctor Reid. The man's pallid flesh was nearly see-through, like fine paper.

"Of course I'm certain. Just fly the ship," the doctor said, his entire body shaking as he took a threatening step toward Delta. He reminded Delta of a chihuahua. "I haven't had to use your chip in some time. Do you need a reminder, is that it?"

"No, sir," Delta said, shaking his head fervently. He hated how he reacted to the threat like a whipped dog, but he was the first to admit that the chip had broken his will. Just thinking about the pain nearly caused him to curl into a fetal position. "I just worry for your safety. The coordinates you gave me are less than a light year from a supermassive black hole. The system is marked as hazardous."

"I'm quite aware of that," the doctor said, waving a hand dismissively. "Get us there. Now."

Delta nodded, moving up the narrow hallway to the

cockpit. He was aware of Reid sitting down next to Kathryn, who'd been increasingly silent since their run-in with Nolan. He wondered how much of the woman remained, and how she felt about betraying a man she'd obviously had feelings for. Delta didn't have much feeling for her one way or the other, but at the very least they were both doing this against their will. That gave them a little common ground.

"Do it, Epsilon," Delta said to the man in the pilot's chair. Well, *man* was a loose term. After the fiasco with Nolan on Coronas 6, Reid had given Delta a new crew, but these new cyber Marines didn't even have names. They might as well have been robots, for all the initiative they showed.

"Yes, sir," Epsilon said mechanically. He had a Marine's buzzcut and a UFC tattoo on his arm. Those were the only clues to the man he'd once been; the rest had been replaced by machinery. Even the man's eyes had been replaced, and Delta knew better than anyone how dehumanizing that was.

The ship rumbled briefly, then began rising through the star's core. This part always bothered Delta. He hated knowing they were under so much pressure, and that if anything failed in the ship's inductive field they'd be incinerated instantly. It made the next several minutes torturous, and he didn't breathe easily again until they'd finally reached the sun's corona.

Massive towers of blue flame rose in pillars all around them, but they were far taller than those on other stars. They stretched hundreds of thousands of miles into the distance, toward a patch of black covering much of the sky. It was like an open wound, completely devoid of stars. The areas around it were rich with twinkling lights, underscoring the darkness.

"This poor star is doomed," Reid said, from right behind Delta. Delta was more than a little surprised he'd not heard the man approaching. "It wandered too close. The black hole's gravity is pulling matter from the sun. We can't see, but the matter is joining a giant accretion disk, the largest in the galaxy. It orbits the black hole, you see. Because the disk is comprised of dark matter, we didn't even know it existed until we explored this system."

Delta nodded, as if that were the most interesting thing he'd ever heard. "Epsilon, make for the coordinates."

The ship's perspective changed, and the viewport showed a different patch of space. It wasn't empty, as there was some sort of planetary body there—a moon, perhaps. It wasn't large enough to be a planet, unless it was further away than he thought. A trickle of ships passed to and from the moon, most of them human, though he saw a few Tigris vessels as well. Those ships had something in common, something that terrified him: they weren't warships. They were cargo vessels and transports.

What the hell were they dropping off?

Delta watched silently, a sense of foreboding growing in the cockpit as they approached the planetoid. The closer they got, the shorter his breaths came. Delta knew, beyond a shadow of a doubt, that his death lay within that planet. It took everything he had not to bolt from the bridge and hide in his bunk.

Part of his mind recognized that the feeling was unnatural, though he had no idea what was causing it. Whatever it was didn't seem to affect Reid, though Epsilon cringed away from the view screen, giving a low whine as he did.

"The Eye," Reid breathed, pushing past Delta and dropping into the *Sparhawk*'s co-pilot seat. He caressed the view screen where the planetoid was, crooning to it. "At long last,

I meet the emissary. I can feel you, hear the whispers. I am home."

The word *horror* could not adequately describe the mix of revulsion and terror that washed through Delta. The object was large enough to make out now. The closer they got, the larger it loomed. It wasn't a planet, though it was roughly spherical. Its surface was milky white, with red veiny sections criss-crossing the surface. An enormous, ropy tail, something like entrails, floated behind the thing. It tapered off into the darkness, writhing slightly as if in an unseen wind.

That wasn't the worst of it, though. The front of the planetoid had an enormous black iris, dilating like a continent-sized whirlpool. Around that iris was a blood-red sea, the thing's cornea. Delta had believed he'd lost the capacity for either wonder or fear, but in that moment he realized how painfully mistaken he'd been. This thing terrified him in a primal way, the kind that aroused fears of the dark in toddlers.

Delta had to look away, so he looked at the pilot's console. It didn't help. If anything, it made the situation worse. The readings were standard for an M-class world. Whatever that thing was, it had a habitable atmosphere.

"Sir, another vessel," Epsilon said, his voice cracking.

Delta saw a flash of metallic blue rising from the monstrous surface. The Primo carrier was clearly headed for the sun, and would just as clearly pass a short distance away from them. "Doctor, how do you want us to proceed?"

"Ignore it," Reid said, waving dismissively. "They are merely feeding the Eye, as are the other vessels. Our mission is far more important."

Delta stared hard at the Eye, and he realized something. Until now, he'd given up. He'd worked blindly for Reid, because he feared the pain. But this...*thing* changed the situation. Whatever it was, Delta believed it could consume the entire human race. Maybe even the Tigris, too.

He didn't know how. He didn't know when. But he was going to find a way to stop that thing.

28

WHAT NOW?

Nolan shifted uncomfortably on his throne, listening to Dryker and Fizgig hash out details. His comm began to vibrate. He ignored it. It vibrated more urgently, so he fished it from his pocket and thumbed on the screen.

"Captain," Ship's cheerful voice said. "I apologize for interrupting you, but Lena said you'd wish to know this immediately."

"Know what?" Nolan asked.

"We've detected Void Wraith signatures lurking in the sun's corona. It is unlikely the Primo would be able to detect them, and I suspect it is the prelude to an attack," Ship explained.

"Stand by," Nolan told Ship. He looked up, pressing the amplifier icon on the throne's right arm. "Everyone listen up." His voice thundered through the room, reverberating off the walls like thunder.

"My ship is picking up Void Wraith drive signatures," Nolan continued, pushing the button to make the throne descend. "We're about to be attacked."

"Our sensors have detected nothing," Celendra said, cocking her head. "Are you certain?"

The others were bringing their thrones back to the dais as well, though the Primo didn't seem to share Nolan's alarm. Nolan leapt from the throne a few feet before it reached the deck, landing in a crouch.

"I'm positive. If you want to live, get your forces into a battle formation. I'm getting back to my ship," Nolan said, turning toward the corridor they'd entered through.

"Nolan, wait," Dryker said, grabbing his arm. "You need a Primo library, right?"

"Yeah," Nolan said, nodding.

Dryker pressed a data cube into his hand. "This has the location of all eight remaining libraries. I suspect they could be under attack as we speak, so you need to be quick. The one at Derinia is the most heavily defended. You might start there."

"Thank you, sir," Nolan said, giving Dryker a tight nod.

"Now get your ass moving. I need to get these Primo ready to fight," Dryker said, turning from Nolan and moving toward Celendra.

"Nolan," Fizgig said. Her tail swished dangerously behind her. "A word."

Nolan approached warily. "What is it, Fizgig? We don't have much time."

"The time has come for us to part ways. I will be joining Khar on the *Claw of Tigrana*. Izzy will be accompanying us," Fizgig said. She placed a paw on Nolan's shoulder. "You have done well these past months. You are one of the rare few with both the talent and the will to act. Keep up your training, and give your life in defense of Lena. She is more important than any of us. Your mission is equally so. Goddess go with you."

"Thank you, Fizgig," Nolan said, giving her a genuine smile. "For everything. I mean that. I'm grateful for your teaching—and you know what? I'm going to miss you."

"To my great surprise, I can say the same. Dryker taught me to respect your race. You have taught me that they can become family," Fizgig said, giving him a respectful nod. From her, that was as good as a hug.

Izzy stood with Annie and Hannan near the mouth of the corridor leading back to the airlock. She and Nolan exchanged a fierce hug, then Izzy moved off to stand with Khar.

The comm vibrated in Nolan's pocket again. "Tigrana watch over you, Fizgig," he said, and trotted down the corridor, Hannan falling smoothly into line behind him. They made great time back to the airlock doors, while Khar, Izzy, and Fizgig split off down another corridor.

"I'm actually a little sad to be losing them," Hannan said, glancing after Izzy. Nolan knew the pair had grown close.

"You know what? Me too, and not just because we'll miss them during the next firefight," Nolan said, slamming the airlock control. He wondered if he'd ever see Fizgig again. He hoped so.

29

RUNNING THE GAUNTLET

"Nolan, do not respond to this transmission," Dryker said, pivoting his throne to face the dome. "It's likely our Void Wraith friends are monitoring this. Don't reveal your location, just get out of here and see to your mission."

The dome showed a wonderful tapestry of the battle, and as Dryker watched, colors and objects began to appear. He realized suddenly that the dome wasn't just decorative. It was functional. The Primo used it to run battles, and the thrones allowed them to move quickly to the area of the battle they wished to study. He was damned impressed.

In this case, the yellow star dominated the view. Their battle group made their way toward the sun, shields at full strength. That was another Primo advantage. Human vessels had the inductive field necessary to survive the stresses of a star, but they required enormous energy to use. That made them impractical for combat. The Primo apparently had a less energy-intensive way of utilizing shields.

"Celendra, how long until we reach the star's corona?" Dryker asked, watching the sun grow larger.

"Just under three minutes," she answered, zooming her throne closer to his. "What do you intend to do?"

"*Claw of Tigrana*, this is Dryker. What's your status?" Dryker asked, ignoring Celendra's question.

"We are well, Dryker," Fizgig's voice answered, confidently. "The vessel is understrength, and we lack the warriors for a sustained battle. We will do what we can."

"Negative," Dryker ordered. "You're to do the same as Nolan, avoid engagement and escape into the star as soon as possible. We need you to reach your people."

"Acknowledged," Fizgig rumbled. "Tigrana watch over you, Dryker."

Dryker didn't reply, instead studying the disposition of the ships. They were in a simple starburst pattern, each close enough to respond if any of the others were attacked. The formation was getting closer to the sun, with no sign of the Void Wraith fleet. Dryker hated not knowing how many enemy vessels were out there, but he was grateful Nolan had provided them any warning at all.

"Celendra, what's the most expedient way to address all vessels at once?" Dryker asked, turning to the Primo. Her large, red eyes studied him.

"You may use the blue button on the far side of the arm. I've just enabled it to our fleetwide broadcast," Celendra said. She paused, then spoke again. "You're aware that they're listening to us."

It wasn't a question, and Dryker didn't bother replying. He didn't have time to teach; he needed to *do*. "Primo fleet, this is Dryker. Odds are good the Void Wraith will attack us as we reach the corona. Slow your advance, and cover each other's flanks."

Dryker toggled the button off, then turned to Celendra. "I want you to ready all offensive weaponry, and every drone this thing can launch. The second you see them de-cloak and attack the *Claw of Tigrana*, I want to destroy the closest Void Wraith vessel."

The distance between the Primo fleet and the *Claw* began to lengthen. Dryker's heart sped as he wondered if he was making the right decision. If he was wrong about Primo reaction time, he might not be able to save the *Claw*. That would be a catastrophic loss, as Fizgig was their only real ally among the Tigris. But this was also their only prayer of drawing the Void Wraith out of hiding, rather than being ambushed by them.

"We are prepared, Admiral Dryker," Celendra finally said. "Seventy-six drones have powered up their reactors. Be aware that this will tax their power level, and they will not be able to fight as long before returning."

"Noted," Dryker said, pivoting the throne to examine the *Claw*. Enough space had opened up that it would take several seconds to close to weapon's range. The *Claw* was close enough to the sun that she would reach the safety of the corona in another sixty seconds.

"Harvesters de-cloaking," Celendra called, a note of panic in her voice. "They're surrounding the *Claw of Tigrana*."

A trio of harvesters rippled into view, each powering up their main weapons. Behind them, three more de-cloaked, these moving to intercept the *First Light*. It seemed they knew who was giving the orders.

"Now, Celendra. Launch everything we have," Dryker said, already broadcasting again before she could respond. "Primo fleet, this is Admiral Dryker. Concentrate all fire on the vessels closest to the *Claw of Tigrana*."

Celendra bore an intense look of concentration, and waves of sleek blue drones began launching from the fighter bays. The tiny, unmanned fighters were each, basically, a plasma rifle bolted to a chassis, with just enough power and intelligence to fight for brief periods.

The drones swarmed the closest harvester, streaks of green energy shooting out in uneven patterns. Because the harvester was firing at the *Claw of Tigrana*, it lacked the power to boost its shields. The first few plasma bursts were shunted harmlessly away, but the rest punched through the shield. Black furrows dug into the pristine blue metal, tearing apart vital systems.

Most of the drones focused on the engines, and after several moments of intense fire, something flared there. The crackling ball of blue plasma the ship had been about to fire changed—fading, then disappearing entirely.

"Witness the power of the Primo, Admiral," Celendra said coldly.

The Primo carrier began to vibrate, a low hum that washed through Dryker's entire body. Then blue-white brilliance poured from the *First Light*. The torrent of energy tore into the already damaged engines, and a massive explosion tore through the back side of the harvester.

The drones continued their assault, focusing on weakened areas. Fires bloomed all along the harvester's hull as internal explosions rocked the ship. She wasn't dead, but she was out of the fight.

"Revenge is sweet," Celendra said, giving a predatory smile.

Dryker ignored her, focusing on the *Claw of Tigrana*. They'd stopped one of the three attacking ships. The other two were still firing.

30

CLAW

F izgig settled into the captain's chair for the first time in months, smiling as she ran her fingers along one of the pillows. Khar hadn't replaced a single one, and there was very little of his fur or scent. Certainly not enough to seep into the fabric. It was as if he'd known she'd be returning, and had used the chair sparingly.

The bridge was woefully understaffed. Izzy was handling communications and piloting, while Khar was manning sensors and weaponry—not that they had much in the way of weaponry. One of the dart tubes had been destroyed, and they only had a handful of darts remaining. There weren't enough crew to man even those few.

Fizgig stared up at the view screen, a welcome change from the holomap on the Void Wraith harvester. The holomap might be tactically superior, but Fizgig had spent decades adapting to the view screen on vessels like the *Claw*. It just felt right.

The screen showed the Primo fleet tightening into a cluster. They were using a simple starburst pattern, which would allow all vessels to react quickly, regardless of what direction they were attacked from. The massive vessels were falling further behind, and as the gap between them and the *Claw* widened, Fizgig gave a broad grin.

"Clever, Dryker," Fizgig murmured. They were being used as bait. "Izzy, order all stations to prepare for imminent attack."

Fizgig was unsurprised when the trio of harvesters shimmered into view around them. She dropped instantly into her old command role, the thrill of combat firing her blood.

"Izzy!" Fizgig roared, rising from her cushioned chair. "Tilt the vessel forty-five degrees along the Z axis. Maximum acceleration."

Izzy responded instantly, and the *Claw* shuddered as it accelerated. If the maneuver worked, the star's gravity would drastically increase their speed, and once they'd broken free of combat they could descend safely into the corona.

If it worked.

"Mighty Fizgig, they're firing," Izzy said, her tail bristling in a very undignified way.

"Stand fast," Khar growled. "We are Tigris. We do not flinch from death."

The *Claw* rumbled in pain, sparks flying from already-damaged systems as the first Void Wraith plasma cannon impacted against the starboard side of the ship. The second hit a moment later, and the lights flickered across the bridge.

"All power to engines," Fizgig said, barely keeping her footing as the ship rocked again.

The *Claw* began pulling away from the harvesters, the gravity of the star whipping the *Claw* like a rock from a slingshot. Both Void Wraith vessels moved to pursue, but several of the Primo carriers had broken off to assist. If they could hold a little while, the Primo would deal with the Void Wraith.

"Mighty Fizgig, shall I deploy darts?" Khar asked, grabbing the railing next to the gunnery station as the *Claw* shuddered dangerously.

"Mighty Fizgig, damage reports coming in now," Izzy said, her words on the heels of Khar's.

Only three of them to man an entire bridge, and even fewer to crew the vessel itself. It seemed unfair, but wasn't that always the way of it?

"How many darts remaining, Khar Prideless?" Fizgig said, rising calmly from the captain's chair. Her tail longed to dash about, but she restrained it to a low, smooth swishing.

"Seven," Khar answered, clearly frustrated by their lack of firepower.

"Do not deploy," Fizgig commanded. She turned to Izzy. "Damage report. Worst areas only."

"We've lost compression along the starboard side of the ship, but as the crew was largely in port, casualties were light. No fatalities," Izzy said. She scanned her data screen for a moment, then looked up to meet Fizgig's gaze. "Our inductive field emitter was damaged. It's only capable of eighty percent strength."

Fizgig allowed herself three deep breaths. She used them to consider the entirety of the situation. The most important factor was escaping the Void Wraith, which meant they had no choice but to dive into the sun. Doing so with hull damage was problematic, though. The weakened inductive field would allow intense radiation through. Unprotected areas of the ship would be melted to useless slag.

"Khar, get everyone to the port side of the core wall, then

seal all bulkheads," Fizgig ordered, knowing she'd be dooming at least a few of her remaining crew that would be unable to escape in time.

Khar began rumbling orders over the comm, face bent low over the communications station next to gunnery. Fizgig was pleased at how quickly he was able to shift from position to position. That kind of versatility was rare, particularly among males his age. He was less rash than most, perhaps as a result of Dryker's tutelage.

"Izzy, how long until the Void Wraith intercept?" Fizgig asked, licking her paw and using it to smooth the fur along her neck. Retaining her composure was the difference between death and victory.

"Two minutes, Mighty Fizgig," Izzy replied. She studied her screen, then spoke again. "Four Primo carriers will close eight seconds after the Void Wraith reach us."

"Dive for the corona. Do it now!" Fizgig roared. She gave a pleased purr as the *Claw* broke for the star's surface. There was no way to stop them from reaching it now. Their allies would have to fend for themselves, but she would reach Tigris space and put an end to Mow. "Tigrana's blessing, Dryker. I've no doubt you'll survive this as you have every other attempt to kill you."

She stared at the view screen, watching the Primo fleet deploy as the *Claw* finally reached the safety of the sun.

31

STAND AND FIGHT

"Celendra, keep us moving toward the rest of the carrier group," Dryker ordered, knuckles going white as he gripped the arms of the throne. He watched the battle unfold, his heart thundering in his chest. Commanding an entire battle was not at all like being in charge of a single ship. His respect for Mendez increased. The old man had made this look easy, until he'd been co-opted by the enemy.

Three harvesters were moving toward the *First Light*. They hadn't even begun cloaking, and instead were warming up their main weapons. Balls of plasma gathered between their wingtips, growing larger before finally discharging.

The first washed harmlessly off the *First Light*'s shield, causing nothing more than a rainbow-colored ripple. The second caused the ship to shudder, and the third tore into the hull in an explosion of blue and white plasma.

"We've lost one of the forward drone bays," Celendra said, dispassionately. Now that the battle had begun, she seemed much calmer.

"Noted," Dryker said, pointing at the closest harvester. "Focus all drones on the lead harvester. Slow it down while we accelerate away. The longer we can keep them chasing us, the more time we give our allies to come to our aid."

Celendra nodded, and the swarm of drones moved to engage the closest harvester. They swarmed around it like bats, firing tiny green beams. The harvester's shield seemed to be holding as it accelerated toward the *First Light*, its two companions not far behind. All three harvesters would be on them before long.

Dryker risked a glance at the far side of the dome. The *Claw* was about to reach the safety of the corona, and the two harvesters pursuing it had finally realized that. They broke off pursuit, pivoting to engage the four Primo carriers that had moved to intercept. Four, not five. Dryker couldn't identify them, so there was no visual way to know which carrier was missing. But Dryker was fairly certain he knew whose it was.

"Celendra, where is Endari's carrier?" he asked, watching as the three harvesters narrowed the gap between themselves and the *First Light*.

"He's broken off from the pursuit of the *Claw*, and is moving in our direction," Celendra said. "Over half our drones have been disabled or destroyed. Our shields are depleted. We are naked before their assault."

Dryker was paralyzed for two agonizing seconds. He knew there were spies among the Primo, or how had the Void Wraith found them? The most likely spy was the one who'd obstinately fought all attempts to unify, the one who made it clear that Primo should never work with the lesser races. Endari. Had he led the Void Wraith to this system?

If Endari were about to betray them, then they were dead. If they changed course to avoid his vessel, then the

Void Wraith would catch them. Hell, the Void Wraith would catch them anyway.

Dryker pressed the blue button, going fleetwide. "Endari, what are you doing?" he asked, trembling as the carrier grew larger in the dome. They'd be in weapons range in a few moments.

Endari's raspy voice finally came over the comm. "The *Claw* is safely away. I thought it prudent to aid you, as these Void Wraith seem intent on your destruction. Accelerate to maximum velocity, and recall your drones. I will deal with these Void Wraith."

"Negative; we'll take them together," Dryker said, a surge of elation running through him. Maybe he'd been wrong about the grey-skinned Primo. Endari's carrier gave them a chance, if a slim one.

"Celendra, you know I am right," Endari said. "We cannot risk losing the *First Light*. Dryker has proved his worth. I admit that I was wrong. For our people to live, Dryker must live. For that to happen, these Void Wraith must be delayed. They seek Dryker's death, for they have realized his importance."

Wave after wave of drones leapt from Endari's carrier. They winged past the *First Light*, engaging the closest harvester. Then Endari's carrier fired its main cannon, savaging the harvester's right wing. The lead harvester withered under the furious assault, slowing to allow its companions to catch up.

"Celendra, bring us about," Dryker ordered.

Celendra ignored him. The *First Light* pivoted, spinning until it dove toward the sun. The other four Primo carriers had broken off and were doing the same.

Dryker stared helplessly as Endari's vessel engaged the three Void Wraith. The withering barrage of plasma fire finally took its toll, and the lead harvester came apart, just like the *Johnston* had only a few months ago. A tear slid down Dryker's cheek as answering fire came from the remaining harvesters. They savaged Endari's vessel, ignoring the drones as they closed for the kill.

The *First Light* descended into the sun's corona, dodging a pillar of flame thousands of miles high. Dryker lost sight of Endari's vessel, and slumped into his seat as the *First Light* made her escape.

Another costly battle.

32

CROSSING THE LINE

Admiral Mendez smiled as he moved to take the captain's chair. He'd taken command of the *Norfolk*, a cutting edge destroyer fresh from the Mars shipyards. There were only four other bridge officers, each connected to their console with a cable that plugged in at the temple. Mendez had greenlit the technology, which hadn't been through standard testing. It linked the prefrontal cortex directly to the ship, making it far more responsive.

All four were chipped, of course. Everyone on the *Norfolk* was, even the Marines. That wasn't true of other Fleet vessels, not yet anyway. Almost a third of the command officers had been chipped, but many of their support staff retained their will. That was being fixed, but it had to be handled delicately.

"Show me the disposition of the Tigris fleet," Mendez demanded. One of the four noncoms shifted the wall-sized display to show a small, orange planet against a tapestry of stars. Little red tags began appearing in orbit around the planet, each denoting a vessel that was far too small to see.

Mendez studied the enemy fleet with mild disbelief. Mow had been true to his word. Tigrana should have had a hundred ships of the line, and there should have been six orbital defense platforms. Instead, there were a scant handful of vessels. Their home world was virtually defenseless.

"Fleetwide," Mendez ordered, clasping his hands behind his back. He waited for the chime that indicated he was live. "Gentleman, today is the day. We are about to take vengeance for this unprovoked assault upon humanity. Show no mercy. Accept no surrender. Turn the cats defending this world into debris, and then prepare for orbital bombardment."

Mendez watched as the 5th, 1st, and 11th tore into the Tigris. The 4th stood by, destroying the few stragglers that made a run for the Helios Gate. It was quick, bloody work. These weren't warriors; they were scavengers. Mow had done his work well. Every fleet-worthy vessel had been removed from Tigrana, and those remaining lacked the leadership necessary to mount an effective defense.

Within minutes, his fleets had destroyed every defending vessel, but the Tigris had clearly spread word to the planet below. Dozens of ships—a collection of civilian transports, freighters, and science vessels—were rising, all fleeing for the imagined safety of the Helios Gate.

"Nothing escapes this system, gentlemen. I want every last ship shot down," Mendez ordered.

He watched as the 4th fleet moved smoothly to intercept the ragtag Tigris ships. It spread over them like a blanket, fires blossoming over a wide swath of space. Not a single vessel made it past the 4th. Every last one was destroyed.

When the short battle was over, Mendez knew it was

time to give the order to bombard the planet. But he didn't, not immediately.

If he did this, he was damning himself. It would cross a line he hadn't yet crossed. Every race had conventions about orbital bombardment. The rule was clear across known space: civilians were off limits.

Fire flooded his spine as he resisted. If he gave this order, it would change the nature of the war. The Tigris would never stop, not until humanity was wiped out. If he ordered the destruction of their home world, one of their races would extinguish the other.

The strategist in him knew which one would lose. The Tigris outnumbered humanity, and they outgunned them. This would whip them into a frenzy, indirectly causing the death of his entire species. Mendez simply couldn't do it.

The fire in his back became acid as the larva made its displeasure known. Mendez bent forward, catching himself against the arm of the captain's chair. The acid spread through his nervous system, overriding his feeble attempts at control. He felt like he was drowning, and when the feeling finally passed he'd lost control of his traitorous body.

"Fleetwide," Mendez said, only a slight tremor in his voice. "Burn that planet, gentlemen. Nothing survives."

33

DERINIA

"Primo library, this is Captain Nolan of the *UFC Johnston*," Nolan began, licking his lips before continuing. "We request permission to approach, and I have to stress that circumstances are urgent. I'm broadcasting footage of the debris field in the Enduria system, where your library used to be. Four other libraries have been confirmed destroyed, and an attack could begin here any minute."

Nolan folded his arms, watching the holographic display that showed the library. It grew larger as they inched closer, waiting for an answer. The crew nervously avoided glancing at each other, as if that might jinx the response from the Primo.

This library was quiet, unlike the last one they'd seen. It bristled with plasma cannons, and a thick blue shield obscured the city-sized structure. Fluted towers rose around a central platform, topped with a dome of shimmering energy that could shelter several Primo carriers. It dwarfed a Tigris orbital defense platform, making this thing the toughest known battle station in existence.

"Such an assertion is ludicrous. Your entire race couldn't damage this library," a flat voice answered. "Yet the laws of hospitality say we must at least hear your baseless tales. Keep your weapons powered down or be destroyed. Make your way to the indicated docking clamp, or be destroyed. Do not deviate from your present course for any reason, or—"

"Be destroyed, yeah we got it," Nolan interrupted. "Listen, I know you're a patient people. I respect that. But you have to be aware of what happened at your conclave. You've probably heard about the other libraries."

There was no answer. Seconds became minutes, but the silence didn't lift. The library grew larger, until it dwarfed the vessel itself. They were getting close.

"Captain Nolan, I will meet you at the airlock door," a second Primo voice said. This one had a different cadence. It was somehow both cultured and weary. "Under the circumstances, you are permitted to bring any armament you may possess."

By the time Nolan's vessel had docked with the station, everyone had gathered at the airlock door. Lena, Hannan, and Annie stood in a little trio surrounding Edwards, who leaned against the wall next to the airlock, trying to pretend he wasn't a twelve-foot-tall robot of death. Seeing them made Nolan miss Izzy, and even Fizgig. Leaving them behind had been tougher than he'd expected. He'd really become fond of Izzy's playfulness, and Fizgig's stern tutelage.

A low hum washed over the ship, and a tingle passed through Nolan's body. Lena giggled, a very odd sound from the Tigris. "We've just passed through the library's protective field. This one was constructed many centuries after the first library we visited, the one the Void Wraith spies blew up. This one is much tougher, which is probably why the Void Wraith haven't tried a direct assault yet."

"Let's hope it's tough enough," Nolan said, glancing at the airlock button as it turned green, indicating a seal had been established on the other side. He tapped it, and the door slid open.

The docking tube was far larger than the ones human vessels used, nearly fifteen feet tall. This was a good thing, as Edwards wouldn't have been able to squeeze into much less.

Hannan took point without a word, gesturing for the others to follow after, defensively. She drew her sidearm as she advanced, but didn't aim it at the figures on the other side of the docking tube.

There were three of them, two wearing the same cere-monial armor Nolan had seen in the previous library. They even used the same archaic war staves, totally impractical for real combat. The third figure wore a snowy white robe, and had deep pink skin. That skin was unlike the other Primo he'd seen, whose skin had been thick and leathery. The coloration ebbed and flowed in mottled patterns.

"She's positively ancient," Lena said, raising a paw to her mouth. "She must be millennia old."

"I'm told it is unkind to speak about age around the elderly," the Primo said, her voice as fragile as she looked. It was the same weary tone Nolan recognized from the comm. "Come, enter Derinia, the largest of our libraries. You may well be our final patrons. We receive very few, these days. What is it you think we can do for you?"

"We're here to—" Nolan began, but the Primo woman cut him off with a sharp gesture.

"I wasn't speaking to you. I was speaking to the scholar," the Primo said, bowing smoothly until her head touched the metal floor near Lena's feet. She straightened, wobbling slightly as she did so. "Ah, the blood rushes to my head. Such an archaic greeting. But I'm rattling on. Welcome to Derinia, little sister. My name is Atrea."

"Little sister?" Lena said, blinking. She gave the widest grin Nolan had ever seen. It was the stuff of a six-year-old's nightmares made real. Damn, but the Tigris had a lot of teeth. "Thank you for receiving us. Time is short, and I'm not entirely certain what I'm seeking. I've prepared a data file with my notes thus far, about the earliest Primo empire."

Lena and Atrea made their way into the library. Hannan eyed Nolan quizzically as he trailed after.

"Sir, what's the objective here?" Hannan said, her voice low. It was largely drowned out by Edwards clomping along behind them. If that weren't enough white noise, Annie rode on Edwards's shoulder, telling him a loud story about ground pounders during the Eight-Year War.

"It's a little muddy," Nolan said, sighing. He met Hannan's gaze, but didn't find the reproach he'd been expecting there. All he saw was trust, with maybe a little respect. "We want a copy of the data core, and Lena knows which parts are important. We just have to hope there's something here that will give us an edge over the Void Wraith. A clue to their identity, or motives. I don't know exactly, but whatever it is...well, it seems like they're going through an awful lot of effort to blow up a few libraries. They have to be afraid we'll learn something they fear."

"Do you want me to keep an eye on Lena?" Hannan asked. Lena and Atrea had moved down the corridor, and would be out of sight soon.

"No, I'll take care of it. I want you to get the full complement of Judicators online," Nolan said, peering back into his vessel. "If trouble shows up, I want to be ready. Hold the dock, and give us an escort back when we're ready."

"Yes sir," Hannan said, nodding respectfully. She paused, moving back to join the others.

Nolan hurried after Lena and the ancient Primo, hoping they could find whatever Lena needed before the Void Wraith arrived.

34

FOOLED YOU

K athryn settled into the co-pilot's chair, buckling herself in out of habit. She was used to piloting the vessel herself, and shot the cyber Marine in the pilot's chair a scornful look. She missed the days when it had been just her and Em, her VI, aboard the *Sparhawk*. But she knew those days were gone forever.

She focused on the library ahead of her, which gleamed under a dome of white-blue light. A tremor of doubt whispered through her, but she ignored it. Their plan was audacious, but given what she knew of the Primo she believed they could pull it off.

"Primo library, this is the *UFC Sparhawk*," Kathryn said, coughing in what she hoped was a convincing manner. "We've taken severe damage, and request assistance. All we need are basic life support repairs, then we'll be out of your hair."

She glanced behind her, finding both her companions. Delta loomed in the doorway, arms folded as he stared at the view screen. His face was impassive as ever, eyes now unreadable pools of silver. That addition was unnerving, as it made it impossible to gauge the man's emotions. Reid was worse, though. He wore his perpetual sneer, equal parts derision and condescension. Combined with his feverish excitement, it made the man positively creepy. It aroused new fear in her. How much of that was his larva? Would her joining carry a similar price?

"Delta, gather your Marines at the airlock door. You're sure this will work?" Reid asked. Again. For at least the fourth time.

"Yes, sir," Delta said, nodding slowly. He was like a beaten dog trying not to get kicked. "The drive is leaking enough radiation to make our story convincing, but not so much that we'll get cooked."

"It has the added side effect of masking our escort," Kathryn said, trying not to snap at Reid. It wouldn't help. "They'll be able to enter when the Primo lower the shield for us."

"Assuming they lower it," Reid said, scowl deepening.

"Oh, ye of little faith," Kathryn said, rolling her eyes. She hadn't dealt much with Primo, but other entities who were connected to the masters had. Through the larva wrapped around her spine she could access some of those memories —those the larva was willing to share, anyway. "Protocol dictates that they render assistance. They can't interfere directly in temporal matters, but they can save lives."

"*UFC Sparhawk*, this is Derinia. Proceed to docking port nine. If you deviate from this course you will be destroyed," the Primo said. He continued layering on threats about what else would get them blown up.

Kathryn only half listened, holding her breath until she felt a sharp tingle. Then she grinned. "We're passing through the shield."

She faced the view screen, which showed the enormous

library beneath them. Two dozen immense plasma cannons were trained on the *Sparhawk*, but thus far they seemed not to suspect anything.

Kathryn blinked when she saw another vessel docked—and not just any vessel, but the unmistakable blue form of a harvester. There was only one harvester actively working against them, which meant Nolan had arrived first. At least he was still here. This sped up their timetable, but as long as they stopped him from leaving they'd stay on schedule.

"Dock as casually as possible," she called into the cockpit, though she knew it was a pointless gesture. The servants Reid surrounded himself with had so much of their body replaced they hardly qualified as people. Delta was the notable exception, though Kathryn was unclear why Reid had made such an exception. Reid did derive quite a bit of pleasure from pushing Delta around, so maybe that was it.

Kathryn turned her attention back to the docking, watching as the *Sparhawk* settled against the library's hull. She turned to Delta. "Okay, this is your show. Get your men ready. I'll take charge of the Judicators. Reid, it's safest if you wait here."

"What if those cannons fire on the ship?" Reid asked, voice rising as he spoke.

"Then you'll be dead before you can reach the airlock door," Kathryn said, turning away from him without another word. She ducked into the mess, then down to the airlock door.

Delta was already waiting there.

"Once all troops are deployed," she said, "link up with me. We'll head for the data core so we can head off Nolan. That has to be why he's here."

35

ATTACKED

Nolan followed Atrea and Lena deeper into the library. The layout was identical to the last one, with corridors stretching off the cavernous main chamber like spokes from a wheel. A series of levels ringed the main floor, each rising toward a domed ceiling that showed the stars. It wasn't unlike the bridge of a Primo carrier, now that he thought about it. This place was many times larger, though.

A handful of Primo wandered between the shelves lining every floor, but Nolan doubted there were more than twenty in all. None looked up as Nolan's group entered; each was enraptured by whatever data cube they were studying. Atrea hurried through the main library room, pausing before a pair of massive double doors. The doors were made of the same blue metal, but unlike the walls they were adorned with vivid scenes of battle, much like the ancient ruins where he and Lena had found the first data cube.

Atrea withdrew a fist-sized signet from under her voluminous robes, fitting the device into the lock set in the middle of the doors. The signet flared a brilliant red, then the doors opened with a click and a hiss of air.

"This is unprecedented," Lena whispered, her tail flicking back and forth excitedly. "No lesser race has ever been allowed to see a master core before."

Atrea strode into the room, circling a wide, black table. A cube roughly twelve feet in diameter floated in the air above the table, though Nolan had no idea what kept it aloft. The cube glowed with its own inner light, a mixture of greens, blues, and whites. The lights changed and pulsed as the cube gently bobbed up and down.

"Please, sit," Atrea said, gesturing at the odd Primo chairs Nolan had still not learned to sit in. "We can use the table to interface with the master cube."

Lena, more graceful than Nolan, settled across the table from Atrea. She was clearly uncomfortable in a chair designed for a race with legs that bent the opposite way, but she mastered it well.

"I am skipping as many of the more tedious formalities as I can," Atrea said, raising a trembling hand to place a jeweled cube in the slot set into the middle of the table. "If you'll tell me why you've come, and what data you wish, I can copy it to this cube."

"I will also try to be brief," Lena said, leaning forward and resting her furry arms on the table. "We have evidence that there were, in fact, three great Primo empires. At some point between the first and second empire, the Primo were genetically modified. The added markers were designed to increase fertility and aggression."

"Hmm," Atrea said, blinking her large, lantern eyes. "I suppose you have evidence to support these claims, but that given the time constraints you will not be able to share it?

Pity. I've long held unpopular notions about the origins of my species, origins that you might be able to substantiate."

"Can you help us?" Nolan asked. "I mean, is there data about the first empire? Or the original Primo DNA?"

"We'll start there," Atrea said, placing both hands on the cube she'd socketed into the table. She closed her eyes and the cube began to glow.

Nolan wasn't sure what she was doing. Was this a ritual, or some sort of Primo ability?

After a moment Atrea looked up. "The data transfer has begun. I'm including all references to the dark times, all information about the genetic drift of our species, and the location of every ancient outpost. What else can I add?"

"Myths," Lena said, rising from the awkward chair and beginning to pace. "Stories of your origins. Parables and the like. Particularly those including the Void Wraith."

"That seems an odd request," Atrea said, cocking her head to the side. "Why?"

"If the data we seek were obvious, then it would have been discovered long ago," Lena said, excitedly. "I believe it may be masked under mythology. There could be real truth buried there, perhaps even the key to unraveling the mystery of the Void Wraith."

"Interesting," Atrea said, giving a single nod. "I'd not have considered that line of thinking. Clearly, I've been correct that we should mingle more with the so-called lesser races. My colleagues would not hear of it, of course. They believe you have nothing to teach. If any of our race survive this, I will make a case to have you appointed a full librarian, little sister."

"That would be wonderful," Lena said, her eyes lighting up. "Why, I—"

The entire library shook. Nolan rose to his feet, drawing

his plasma pistol as he scanned their surroundings. They were in the safest place they could be, locked in the vault at the heart of the library. A second shudder rocked the station, this one more violent than the first.

"What's happening, Atrea? Do we have a way to find out?" Nolan demanded.

"Yes, yes...give me just a moment," Atrea said. She pointed at Nolan's comm. "You can now access the library's security cameras."

Nolan swiped the screen several times until he arrived at a camera on the edge of the library. His heart sank when he realized what he was seeing. Two Void Wraith harvesters had just rammed the station, and were no doubt dumping full compliments of Judicators inside.

How the hell had they gotten past the Primo's shields? So far as he knew, harvesters possessed nothing that would let them ignore a field of that strength. Nolan's gaze landed on a smaller ship, and he choked back a curse. A Photos-class vessel had just docked, and he was positive he knew which one. That had to be the *Sparhawk*.

Kathryn had arrived.

He looked up at Lena and Atrea. "We need to leave, right now."

36

BOO

Dryker clasped his hands behind his back, staring out the Primo dome. Dozens of tiny freighters flitted from Ceras Station out to the three colonies in this system. All three were terraformed for one purpose: to provide food for the entire periphery. Nearly every outer colony depended on this station for its very survival, especially during the early years when they were getting established.

Ceras Station was close to the sun, a mere million miles above the surface. Keeping it that close meant the station had to move actively to avoid coronal mass ejections from the star, so it possessed more thrusters than he'd ever seen a station have. Ceras was also larger than anything he'd seen outside the core worlds, large enough to hold ten thousand citizens.

Behind it he could see two of the three worlds that had been terraformed in the system. New Mars was a red world, though due to its size, the gravity was higher even than Earth. Most of the terraformers who'd colonized the world never left it again. Vega was a small blue world, roughly two-thirds the size of Earth. Its beaches made it a perfect vacation spot, one Dryker had visited twice during his time in the UFC.

"Why have we journeyed to this system, Admiral Dryker?" Celendra asked, gliding up to join him. She somehow made the awkward Primo gait elegant.

"If mankind had an official capital of the periphery, Ceras would be it," Dryker replied, glancing briefly at her before returning his gaze to Ceras Station. "They're the second-richest corporation in human space."

"So you come seeking money?" Celendra asked, her confusion evident. She opened her mouth to speak again, then closed it, shaking her head.

"I'm sorry, Celendra. I haven't been very good at explaining myself," Dryker said, turning to give the Primo his full attention. "I've been too focused on keeping us alive, and haven't spared the time to properly explain. We came to Ceras because they have a contract with the 14th fleet. Their donations account for sixty percent of the 14th's funding. When Ceras calls, the 14th fleet comes running."

"Ahhh," Celendra said, giving a smile made comical by her tiny mouth. "So you will call the 14th fleet to this place, and attempt to win them to our cause."

"That's the plan," Dryker said, reaching for his comm. Thanks to the Primo, it was now linked to the Quantum Network. It still terrified him how easily the Primo had done that. "If we're lucky, one of the Ceras higher-ups is on station right now. If I were her, and I saw a Primo battlegroup enter the system, how do you think I might react?"

"We're picking up several communications coming from the station," Celendra said, looking out the dome at the station. "One of them is utilizing heavy encryption. Ahh, there we go. I've decrypted the data stream, and will play the audio."

"—get your ass here now," a woman snarled, in exactly the kind of tone that knew it would be obeyed. "I don't care how drunk your officers are, or who's locked up in some local prison. You get every ship in your fleet to Ceras in the next eight hours, or we find another fleet to sponsor next year."

"I can't just strip the periphery," a tired voice answered. A familiar voice. "I'll get four capital ships there in the next few hours, but—"

"But nothing," the female voice snarled. "You'll—"

"I apologize for interrupting your call," Dryker said, maybe a little too cheerily. It wasn't every day that disgraced captains showed up with a Primo fleet under their command, and damned if he wasn't going to showboat a little. "This is Admiral Dryker, and I'm in command of the Primo fleet orbiting Ceras."

"Jim?" the male voice said. "Is that really you?"

"How did you crack this encryption?" the woman roared, drowning them both out.

"Lady, I don't really need you on this call," Dryker said. His time for putting up with corporate bureaucrats was past. "I needed to talk to the acting head of the 14th fleet, and you just put me in touch with him. The Primo aren't going to harm Ceras. You can go back to your wine party."

"Ceras will censure you. You'll be stripped of your rank," the woman sputtered.

Dryker ejected her from the call, making doubly sure her icon had disappeared before he spoke again. "Jamison, I need to ask you a favor. I want you to reach out to captains you trust, no more than a handful. We need the influential people, like Sheng. The ones who can get the rest of the fleet on board with the craziest idea they've ever heard."

"Why? And what the hell are you doing in command of a Primo battlegroup?" Jamison said. There was no heat to his voice, just confusion. Maybe a little excitement.

"Because the war with the Tigris is a smokescreen," Dryker said. He paused to give Jamison a chance to respond, but the man said nothing. "Most of the Primo have been wiped out by the same people who've made a third of the periphery go dark. They're called the Void Wraith, and they've got us fighting the cats to weaken both sides. When the war is over, they'll sweep in and mop up whoever is left."

"Okay, let's say I buy this. Why do you want to gather the 14th? We're the *underfunded* 14th, remember? We don't have the manpower or resources to make a difference. Our whole fleet wouldn't be the equal of one of your carriers," Jamison protested, more than a little bitterly. Like most captains in the 14th, he'd been ground down under years of frustration. They were given an impossible job and next to no resources, then left to flounder.

"Because I can outfit the 14th with Primo weaponry," Dryker said, his smile leaking into his voice. "Are you interested?"

37

REFITTED

Dryker sat down with Juliard, the last member of the *Johnston's* crew to stick with him. She slid deeper into the booth, all but sinking into the torn leather. The short blonde looked like a toddler at the oversized table. Dryker slid in next to her, surveying the bar. He'd been to McMalley's half a dozen times over the years, and rarely remembered the trip back to his ship. He definitely remembered the hangovers, though.

"Do you think they'll show?" Juliard asked, taking a sip of her beer. She scanned the twenty or so patrons suspiciously.

"They'll show, but in their own time," Dryker said, savoring a mouthful of terrible soy beer. At least it was cold. The Primo served all their food at room temperature. "They're probably having a separate meeting right now. They'll settle things amongst themselves, then come to meet us."

"I think we're being watched," Juliard said, looking pointedly down at the table. "There's a man in a blue shirt next to the door, and another seated at the table two over from us. Both have been staring."

Dryker glanced at both men from the corner of his eye, running a quick threat assessment. Then he started to laugh. When Juliard's shocked face turned up to him, he laughed harder. It took several wheezing breaths to bring the laughter under control.

"What the hell do you find so funny?" Juliard hissed. "Now everyone is staring at us."

"Lieutenant, the men you indicated were staring at *you*, not at us," Dryker said, struggling to catch his breath. He shook his head, still smiling. "When was the last time you were in a bar?"

"I don't really do bars," she said, glaring at the men who'd stared at her. Both looked back at their drinks.

"Here they come," Dryker said, straightening, then giving a wave.

Jamison returned the wave, then led a cluster of hard-faced men and women over to the booth. He slid in next to Dryker, and the rest of the captains all slid in after. The booth was elbow-to-elbow by the time everyone had sat down.

"Sheng, Smith," Dryker said, nodding to the two he recognized. The former was a Chinese woman in her late sixties, the latter a brick of a man in his early forties.

"Dryker, meet Hawk, Brenner and Nagabushan." Jamison gestured at each in turn. "The rest you've already met. I told the boys—"

"There are three women here," Sheng interjected.

"I told the *crew*," Jamison said, correcting himself, "that you'd be paying our bar tab, and that all they needed to do was listen."

"That's the deal. Have a seat, and order whatever you want. It's all on my tab. Drink liberally, because my plan is terrible and that will make it sound better," Dryker said. He reached into his jacket, setting six cylinders on the table. "Each of you take one of these back to your ship. It contains footage showing the battle in the Ghantan system, plus the circumstances leading up to it."

"That's the battle where the *Johnston* bought it, right?" Brenner, one of the few Aussies in the 14th, asked. "Brass said you bought it too, along with most of the 7th."

"That's the battle," Dryker said, a knife twisting in his chest at the mention of the *Johnston*. "The brass is full of shit though, even more so than usual. The whole thing is a cover-up. They lied about what happened, and you're holding the proof."

If Dryker had said that to a table full of captains in any other fleet, odds were good he'd have been on the receiving end of the world's most enthusiastic ass kicking. The 14th was different, though. They knew they were the red-headed stepchildren of Fleet, and that if the top brass were involved, then the 14th was getting screwed again.

"This is the part that's going to be hard to swallow, and before you react I want you to remember that there is evidence proving it on those data drives I passed out," Dryker said. He took a deep breath, and said the thing that would make or break his case. "The whole conflict with the Tigris is a smokescreen. Higher-ups in both their fleet and ours have colluded to start a war."

Absolute silence at the table. Bad country music continued to play in the background. A woman laughed raucously as her date told a joke. Finally, Jamison licked his lips and spoke. "Why would they do that?"

"This one goes deep," Dryker said, leaning in close and lowering his voice. "They want to bleed both fleets, to keep us weak so we're easy to conquer. The people doing this just wiped out most of the Primo fleet. The rest of it? That's parked on the other side of this system, ready to help us take it to the real enemy in this war."

"Let's say we're willing to believe this—and I'm not saying we are." Sheng eyed him dubiously. "Who is this enemy, and what do you expect the 14th to do about it? Throw rocks? We're not equipped for a full war. We're a bunch of ancient ships put out to pasture. We police pirates, and barely have the ordinance to do even that much."

"You already know the answer, or I doubt Jamison would have convinced you to come," Dryker said. He pulled his plasma pistol from its holster and set the weapon on the table.

Sheng grinned at him. That grin spread to every face at the table.

"I've got twenty of these for every captain that signs. Your Marines will have the edge over everyone they fight," Dryker said, leaning back in his seat. He savored another mouthful of beer while they passed the pistol around. "That's not all I can offer, though. Hand-to-hand is one thing, but we're going toe-to-toe with capital ships. Your vessels need some extra punch there, too. We have Primo assault cannons, and using their tech, we can bolt them to your hulls. It won't be pretty, but you'll have access to plasma weaponry."

"Come on guys," Sheng said, elbowing Brenner, and waiting for everyone to look at her. "Yeah, I know the gun is shiny. I want them, too. Let's be real for a moment first. If we sign on, what do you plan to do? Are you going to attack our own vessels?"

"Just one of them," Dryker said, leaning over the table to stare hard at Sheng. "The admiralty put us here. Mendez, Chu...probably all of them are working against us. Once the 14th is up to speed, we're going to hunt them down."

38

PRIDE LEONIS

"Open a channel to the fleet," Fizgig ordered, composing herself on her chair. She'd piled the pillows artfully around her, demonstrating the kind of comfort every captain strove for.

"We're broadcasting, Mighty Fizgig," Izzy said, giving her a deferential nod. Izzy's snowy fur was pristine, though it hadn't been, until Fizgig had chastised her about her grooming. Most prideless didn't understand how important appearances were when determining pride standing.

"Leonis Pride, hear me," Fizgig said, making her words bold and powerful. She stared into the view screen, unblinking. "I am Mighty Fizgig of the *Claw of Tigrana*. I have come to challenge Mow for leadership of the pride. Under the auspices of Tigrana, I will prevail."

Fizgig made a gesture, and Izzy stabbed a button on her console. The view screen shifted back to a view of the Leonis fleet orbiting the Tok Shipyards.

"Hah," Khar said, giving a rumbling chuckle. Then he began to purr. "Let us see what they make of that."

Fizgig's tail swished, her only reply. Tradition dictated

how this would unfold. None of the other captains would speak to her until Mow had replied. If Mow didn't reply, vessels would flock to her. She'd neatly pinned the old cat. Either Mow faced her, or he lost his fleet.

"I am pleased to see you live," Mow's voice said. The view screen flared to life, showing the bridge of his vessel. "I am less pleased that you would choose the eve of battle to challenge me, especially after having been gone so long. Many questions remain, Fizgig. Where have you been? Why have you returned now? I will not allow you to sow discord among our ranks."

"You know where I've been, and why," Fizgig said, rising gracefully from her pillows. She approached the screen, knowing that every captain in the system was watching their conversation. "You orchestrated this war based on a lie. The humans were not responsible for the destruction of our fleet in the Ghantan system. I was there, Mow. And I have proof."

Mow leaned back into his own pillows, his tail swishing lazily. "Really? Then how do you explain this?"

Mow gestured, and a window opened up on the corner of the screen. It showed the battle in the Ghantan system— or a part of it anyway. It was from the perspective of the Tigris vessels, and it showed them being fired upon by a human fleet. The camera showed nothing of the Void Wraith—not their harvesters, their factory, nor their bomb.

So far as this footage suggested, there'd been a battle between humans and Tigris, one the humans had clearly won. Fizgig's tail sank a good two inches before she willed the descent to stop. She stiffened, meeting Mow's gaze.

"I possess similar footage, but mine shows the *true* battle. Khar, display our battle recording from Ghantan," she ordered, waving a paw in Khar's direction.

"Yes, Mighty Fizgig," Khar said, bending to the task. A

moment later, the small window in the corner of the screen returned, this time with her version of the battle.

"Notice the strange blue vessels. They are the Void Wraith," Fizgig said, triumphantly. "As you can see, they are destroying the human vessel, the *Johnston*. You can also see their factory, and the bomb they intended for Theras Prime. The human fleet was controlled by agents of the Void Wraith."

"A pretty story," Mow said, his tail still swishing haughtily.

Fizgig recoiled as if struck.

"How can we verify any of this from your footage?" Mow asked. "Clearly there is some new race, but that new race is working *with* the humans. The *Johnston* was a rogue vessel. They were probably trying to alert us to the humans' own treachery."

"I have all the evidence needed to prove my claims, and I am broadcasting it to the fleet as we speak," Fizgig said, stalking toward the screen. She glared up at Mow. "You cannot run, Mow. I will hunt you down, and I will tear out your throat with my own fangs. I promise you that."

"Will you?" Mow said, rather smugly. Then his expression grew more solemn. "I will give you one chance to survive, Fizgig. One chance to prove that you value your people over the deceiving humans. I've just received word that your precious humans are assaulting Tigrana."

"Tigrana can hold off any human assault. Even a single orbital platform would devastate anything the humans possess," Fizgig said, her eyes narrowing to slits. "What are you playing at, Mow?"

"The prides convened, and we moved the defense platforms to front-line worlds," Mow admitted, eyes glittering.

He knew he had her, and that she knew it. "It was a general vote, and passed almost unanimously."

Fizgig froze. For the first time in two decades, she didn't know what to do. Visions of her world burning filled her mind. The humans raining death on the unprotected Imperial Academy where her four grandkits went to school.

"What about the fleets?" Fizgig asked, agonized. "At least two prides watch over our world; that is the covenant." Her niece was about to graduate from the Royal Academy, the first scientist in three generations. Her sister wrote Fizgig about it daily, so often that Fizgig could scarcely keep up.

"Stripped, to battle the humans," Mow admitted, giving a heavy sigh. "Again, not my doing. It was voted on by the prides. So you see, Fizgig, we must set aside our squabble for the good of the Tigris. We must save our home world, which is even now under siege by humans."

Fizgig's tail topped to the floor, and this time she didn't stop it. There was nothing she could say or do to unseat Mow, not if the humans were really assaulting Tigrana.

39

BATTLE LINES

Hannan instinctively checked her weapon's action, realizing for the hundredth time that Void Wraith tech had no action. The plasma rifle was, for all intents and purposes, a single piece of metal. Its internals were completely covered in artfully crafted curves. The weapon was lightweight, didn't ever seem to heat up, and took several hundred shots to drain.

"Sarge, did you feel that?" Edwards rumbled, clomping his metallic frame to the head of the line of much shorter Judicators clustered around him.

"'Course she felt it," Annie said, spitting a gob of black over the railing and into the darkness below the walkway. "The dead felt that."

The ship shuddered again. Hannan straightened. "Those are impact tremors. Just like the ones we felt aboard the *Johnston* before we were boarded."

"What do you want to do, Sarge?" Edwards asked, shifting from foot to foot. The Judicators around him all took a step back.

"Someone or something found their way past the Primo

defenses. Looks like you'll finally get a chance to show off, Edwards," Hannan said, walking over and slapping Edwards's leg. "We're going to make for the center of the library. Our goal is to extract Nolan and hightail it back to the ship. Edwards, you're going to hold the main library room with the smaller Judicators. Annie and I will get to Nolan, then we'll fall back to you. Everyone know what to do?"

Annie snapped a tight salute, as did Edwards. A moment later, the Judicators all did the same. Not in unison, but as if each were figuring out for themselves that it was the correct gesture. Jesus, these things learned quickly. Were they all like Edwards, but unable to speak?

"Let's move," Hannan said, shoving down the extraneous thoughts. She didn't have time for philosophy.

They trotted up the corridor, a wide hallway that Edwards had no problem navigating. It went on for a good two hundred yards, then opened into a tactical nightmare. There were multiple levels filled with rows of densely-packed shelves. Those would make great cover, and give endless places for snipers to hide. The main room wasn't any better. The tables could be used for hard cover against low targets, but anyone on the upper floors would just fire right over them.

"Captain, this is Hannan," she said into her comm.

"Go ahead, Sergeant," Nolan's voice crackled back.

"We've moved to the central room, and are about to secure it. Where are you in relation to us?" Hannan asked.

"I'd rather not reveal that, even on an encrypted channel," Nolan replied. "Secure the main room and we'll find our way to you."

"Smart, sir," Hannan said. "Hannan, out."

She turned to Edwards.

"I want you to take up a position at the far side of the room, between those shelves. Get low if you can, and sit overwatch on the passages leading into this room. It looks like all entrances come to the first floor." Hannan scanned the layout as she spoke. "Judicators, listen up. I need alpha squad up to the fourth level, beta on third, and kappa on second. Annie, you and I will provide ground-cover fire for Edwards."

"Yes, sir," Annie said, trotting after Hannan into the corner of the library, between two shelves. They took up positions about fifteen feet from each other, their fields of fire overlapping to cover the midsection of the room.

"Sir, should I engage cloak?" Edwards called, loudly.

"Yes," Hannan hissed back. "And keep your voice down."

Hannan wished Lena had had the time to tinker on the Judicator tech. She'd have given a lot for a portable cloaking device similar to what the Judicators wore. They provided one hell of a combat advantage, and were the primary reason she'd made sure all the snipers were Judicators. It was damned hard to deal with a bunch of invisible snipers.

Something shimmered at the mouth of one of the tunnels. Hannan was still snapping her rifle to her shoulder when a flurry of shots streaked down from the upper levels. The first blast rippled across an invisible target. The second and third dissipated the shield, and the fourth and fifth reduced the Judicator to scrap and goo.

"Edwards, wait to engage," Hannan whispered, using the comm this time.

She sank into a crouch, waiting for several tense breaths. Then shimmering forms started sprinting through the opening, into the main room. There were dozens of them, all nearly impossible to track. The only indication was the heat shimmer.

The air filled with plasma blasts from both sides as the Judicators began firing at each other. She glanced at Annie, noting that the soldier was eyeing the combat, but hadn't yet fired. Good. It was nice to know she had discipline and could follow orders.

"Now," Hannan whispered into the comm. She leaned forward, taking aim at one of the heat shimmers, and fired, bracing instinctively for the kick that never came. The lack of kick was the hardest adjustment she'd had to make in adapting to the alien weaponry.

Her shot caught the Judicator in the leg, its form shimmering into view as it cartwheeled into the side of a table. Before it could rise, Edwards stepped from cover. He darted forward, crushing the Judicator's head with the heel of his foot. Edwards pivoted, aiming one of the plasma cannons underslung along his arms. It fired a huge burst of blue fire, melting another Judicator into unrecognizable slag.

"Woohoo," Edwards yelled. "This thing is *awesome!*"

Then the Judicator under Edwards's foot detonated, launching Edwards into a shelf thirty feet behind him. His metal body crushed the shelf, shattering dozens of data cubes as it crashed to the floor. Hannan compartmentalized the combat, still firing at Judicators as she considered the implications.

Some of the Judicators exploded, but only ones near strategic targets. It was as if there were someone watching the combat, and only blowing up the ones that helped their cause. That was new, and more than a little alarming.

Hannan gunned down another Judicator, then another. It was a hell of a lot easier to do with a plasma rifle. Beside her, Annie was doing the same. They'd been ignored thus far, as the enemy Judicators struggled to deal with the snipers above.

The shelf next to Hannan ceased to exist, its smoldering remnants raining down around her. She looked up, eyes widening. "Edwards, stop screwing around. Someone in your weight class just showed up. Enemy Alpha, eleven o'clock."

40

SAVING A CULTURE

Nolan unholstered his plasma pistol, peering through the double doors. He could hear plasma fire in the distance—an uncomfortable reminder that, if the Judicators broke through, they'd be on the master core in moments.

"Atrea, how's it coming in there?" Nolan called over his shoulder. Atrea and Lena were clustered around the cube set into the table, bathed by the glow of the master cube above.

"I am saving the vital essence of an entire culture," Atrea snapped, her outstretched hands pressed against either side of the cube. "Do not rush me."

"We might have enough, if we need to leave," Lena said, creeping to the doorway and crouching across from Nolan. She pulled out a plasma pistol of her own, though Nolan had never seen her fire it. "If we can wait another few minutes, we'll be saving countless things that could help us. Since we don't know precisely what we're after, I'd recommend letting Atrea work as long as possible."

Nolan considered his answer. How long could they

afford to stay? Sixty seconds? A hundred and twenty? How did he weigh the risk versus the potential reward?

"She can have three minutes, then we're pulling out," Nolan said.

"Okay," Lena said, ears drooping. "I will let her know."

Nolan continued to scan the corridor leading back to the library's main room. Seconds passed, then a full minute. He almost missed the slight shimmer, and it was only a few feet away by the time he reacted. He fell back a pace instinctively, and the motion saved his life.

A plasma blade flared into existence, descending toward his face in a tight arc. It whizzed through the space Nolan had just occupied, humming so close to his face that he could see individual whirls of superheated particles in the beam.

Nolan snapped his wrist forward, igniting his own blade. He lunged forward, ramming it toward where he thought the enemy's chest might be. The disembodied plasma blade snapped up to block, knocking his own aside.

A flash of blue streaked by overhead, then two more in rapid succession. Nolan risked a glance behind him, wincing when the saw the target. More and more plasma blasts streaked into the master core, until it finally shuddered and went dark. Whatever force had been holding it in place disappeared, and the cube plummeted toward the table. Nolan sprinted into the room, diving for Atrea. He tackled her out of the way as the cube crashed down where she'd been standing.

"Put your weapons down, Nolan," Kathryn's voice called from up the corridor. "You're outnumbered, and we'd prefer to take you alive."

Four figures shimmered into view as Nolan rose to his feet. Nolan recognized Delta immediately, though the other two cyber Marines were new. All three held plasma rifles, and both Delta and the Marine who'd assaulted Nolan had plasma blades. They were armed with Void Wraith tech, and Nolan guessed the belts accounted for the cloaking fields.

"Captain, we must not let them take the cube," Atrea said, groaning as she rose shakily to her feet. "It is all that remains of the master cube."

"Not helping," he said, his eyes never leaving the Marine in front of him. The cyber Marine had taken two steps closer, his plasma blade raised.

If Nolan excelled at any one thing, it was analysis. That was the reason he loved all things tactical—from video games to chess to ship-to-ship combat. He knew how to read a situation, and his read on this one left no room for escape. Kathryn had him dead to rights, and if he tried to fight back all three of them would die. The best he could hope for here was a slight delay, something to buy time for Hannan's squad.

"Before I surrender, I need answers, Kathryn," Nolan said, still watching the Marine. "Why are you doing this? Why are you selling out your race?"

"I'm sorry, Nolan," she said, and from her tone Nolan thought she might actually mean it. "You'll understand soon enough. What's coming is inevitable, and the best way to minimize the loss of life is to give the masters what they want. I'll only say it one more time. Lower your plasma blade. We'd rather not kill you."

Nolan flicked his wrist, and the blade winked out. Despair clutched at his heart. He was out of options, and judging from the frantic plasma fire in the distance, Hannan was in no position to help.

41

ALPHA DUEL

Edwards wasn't the smartest guy ever to enlist; he knew that. That was part of what had landed him in the 14th to begin with. He rarely knew the right thing to do, unless the right thing was bashing an enemy into submission. Unfortunately, his understanding of when that should happen didn't line up with his COs'—until he'd met Hannan.

The shift from being a flesh-and-blood Marine to a giant killing machine hadn't really changed Edwards much. It just changed how other people looked at him. Before, they'd tried to restrain him. Now, they pointed him at things they wanted dead. It was his favorite part of being an Alpha.

"I love this job," Edwards said, leaping twenty feet into the air. Streaks of plasma zipped past him, from above and below. One even hit his right foot, scoring the metal but not causing him any pain or discomfort. Edwards took aim at the Judicator who'd fired, its form hunched behind a table. He fired a single burst, and his target simply exploded.

He landed in a crouch behind a shelf, then popped up over it to fire at another pair of Judicators. Both died messily.

"My favorite part is that all that cloaking crap you do doesn't work on me."

Edwards pivoted to face another pair of Judicators.

"Guess what? I can see you." Two more casualties.

"Edwards, stop screwing around," Hannan's voice echoed in his head via the comm. "Someone in your weight class just showed up. Enemy Alpha, eleven o'clock."

Edwards felt a stab of uncertainty, for the first time since he'd woken up in this body. What if the enemy Alpha was a better fighter? If it took him out, the rest of the squad was toast.

So he needed to win. Sarge wanted that thing dead, and Edwards was going to go kill it.

He sprinted along the library's outer ring, kicking aside tables as he circled the room. It didn't take long to spot the other Alpha. It used one hand to fire into the area where Annie and Hannan had taken shelter, and the other to suppress the sniper fire raining down from above.

"Hey, ugly!" Edwards roared, pounding across the library floor toward the other Alpha. "These things come with plasma swords. You wanna have a go?" Edwards ignited the blade built into his left arm, skidding to a halt amidst the wreckage caused by exploding Judicators and plasma fire.

The other Alpha turned toward Edwards. It paused for a second as if considering, then extended its right arm. An identical plasma blade appeared, and the Alpha began stalking toward Edwards. As it approached, a smaller Judicator walked in front of it, and the Alpha swatted it aside like a puppy. The Alpha pointed at Edwards, then beckoned with its free hand.

"Guess becoming a robot don't strip away pride," Edwards said, wishing he had a mouth to grin with. He strode forward, launching a brutal strike at the other Alpha. It knocked his blade away, swiping at his side. The blade cut through his armor, exposing circuitry covered in orange fluid.

So Edwards punched the Alpha in the face. The move caught his opponent off balance, and in that split second Edwards charged up the rifle underslung along his arm. The enemy Alpha tried to take a step back, but it was far too late. Edwards fired, melting its head to slag. The Alpha collapsed to the floor.

"Yep, definitely love this job."

"Edwards, I've got two more heavies moving into the room. Move your ass," Annie screeched over the comm.

Edwards turned in time to take a blast to the chest that launched him into the shelf behind him. He didn't feel any pain, but the red areas on the HUD were terrifying. That shot had done some real damage.

42

DIDN'T SEE THAT COMING

"You've got me dead to rights," Nolan sighed, holstering his pistol. Beside him, Lena did the same.

Kathryn advanced, lowering her own weapon. She smiled at Nolan. "I'm so glad you're willing to cooperate. I promise that very soon you'll understand that you've been fighting on the wrong side."

Nolan was completely unprepared when Delta pressed his plasma rifle to the back of a cyber Marine's skull, and fired. The Marine's head simply ceased to exist, and his lifeless body tumbled to the ground.

That triggered several things at the same time.

Lena leapt to the shattered remains of the table, yanking the data cube out of the socket. The second Marine, the one who'd attacked Nolan, swung his plasma blade at Delta. Finally, to Nolan's surprise, he found himself lashing out with his foot, catching Kathryn in the knee.

She rolled with the blow, staggering backwards and igniting a plasma blade. He should have expected she'd have one. Nolan brought his own blade into a guard position, easing his pistol out of its holster with his other hand.

Kathryn glided forward, darting like a viper when she was within range. Nolan barely managed to block, knocking the blade aside, and backpedaling into the room. Kathryn pursued, keeping pressure on him, just like Fizgig would have. One of her first lessons had been: *don't give ground, unless you have a reason.*

Nolan did. "Lena, shoot Kathryn."

Kathryn's gaze darted toward Lena, whose hands were busy stuffing the data cube into her satchel. It only took Kathryn a split second to recognize the deception, but Nolan made good use of the time. He swiped low at Kathryn's belly, and as he'd expected, she hopped back a step to avoid the blow.

Nolan raised his pistol and fired a gob of plasma at her chest. The shot knocked her prone, but he'd used a low enough setting that he knew it hadn't killed her. Still, he shot her once more for good measure. It was best not to take chances, not with this much at stake.

"Done," Lena said, tucking her arm through the satchel's strap.

Nolan glanced at Delta, who was wrestling with the last Marine. Delta ever-so-slowly forced the man's own blade down, grunting with effort until he plunged the weapon into his opponent's heart. The Marine twitched, then lay still.

Kathryn's form suddenly moved, lunging forward and planting her blade into Nolan's leg. Every muscle seized up at once, and he collapsed into a twitching pile. Before Kathryn could capitalize on the attack, Atrea stepped up and fired a plasma pistol into her face. Kathryn collapsed next to Nolan, twitching in the exact same way he was.

"That's for what you did to the master cube," Atrea

snarled, then knelt next to Nolan. She raised a small blue device, passing it over the area where he'd been stabbed. "She'll be all right in a moment. I'd recommend restraining her. She wasn't trying to kill you. There's almost no cellular death. You were lucky."

Feeling returned to Nolan, and he struggled into a sitting position. "Why didn't she stay down after I shot her?"

"I believe the device they're using as a cloaking field also provides them limited protection against plasma weaponry," Atrea said. She unclipped Kathryn's belt and handed it to Nolan. "We've long theorized that a personal protective field would be possible, but our only hand-to-hand combat is ceremonial, so no one has bothered to test the application."

Nolan staggered to his feet, rubbing his temple. Blinding white pains still shot through him every few seconds, but he was more or less functional. He turned to face Delta, who waited impassively for Nolan's attention. This was going to be an awkward conversation, one they didn't have time for. "Delta, we can talk about details later, but for now I'm assuming you're with us?"

"That I am," Delta said, licking his lips. His chest was still heaving from the combat. "We need to get out of here fast, before Reid figures out I'm not his puppet. The moment that happens, he'll yank my strings again. I want to be far away from here when that happens."

"We're just as eager to get out of here. Give me a second," Nolan said, then raised his comm. "Hannan, give me a sit rep."

"Sir, now's not a great time," Hannan called back. Something detonated in the background. Plasma fire sounded all around her. "We need to get out of here, and quick. We're getting the worst of this fight."

"Give us forty seconds," Nolan said, clipping Kathryn's stealth belt around his waist.

43

HANNAN

Hannan sized up the combat, swearing under her breath. "Annie, shift your fire to the south corridor entrance. Keep it as clean as you can."

Annie continued to impress Hannan; she was an economical soldier who knew how to follow orders. Hannan watched as she moved in a low sprint from one shelf to the next, ducked behind a table, then let out a burst of plasma that dropped a Judicator.

"We've got trouble, Sarge."

It didn't take Hannan more than a split second to spot the 'trouble.' A flood of enemy Judicators had rushed both stairwells, and were forcing their way to the second level. They burst out, using superior numbers to overwhelm the snipers Hannan had left in place. That reduced the cover fire from above, which allowed more Judicators to reach the stairwells.

"Captain, this is going south," she called into her comm. "You'd better run faster."

Hannan ducked as Edwards sailed overhead, smashing two Judicators flat. Both detonated a moment later, launching Edwards back into the air with an explosion of concussive force. Hannan braced herself behind cover, and when she glanced out again her heart sank. One of Edwards's arms had been severed, and there was exposed circuitry along his chest and right leg.

"Private, can you hear me?" she yelled into the comm.

"Sure can, Sarge," Edwards called back, cheery as ever. He began crawling to his feet, using one of the last remaining shelves as cover. "I don't think I can take too much of this punishment, though. I did for those two Alphas, but if they send another one I think we're in real trouble."

"Annie, how's that south corridor looking?" Hannan yelled, popping from cover long enough to blow the leg off a Judicator.

"Not too rosy," Annie yelled back, pausing to fire another volley. "They're not coming out of the tunnel, but I think they've figured out we're trying to reach it."

"Shit," Hannan said. She looked at the east corridor, where all the Alphas had come from. The heat shimmers were layered thickly around the door, and she was betting they were massing for another assault. "Edwards, the second you see the captain, I want you to bull rush every Judicator between us and the south corridor."

"Yes, sir," Edwards yelled back, sticking his remaining arm from cover and firing wildly. She couldn't see if he hit anything, but the answering volley of plasma shots put several head-sized holes in the shelf Edwards was sheltering behind.

Hannan took a look at the levels above, cringing. The enemy Judicators were clearing the third floor. They'd be on the fourth floor in moments, and that meant the wonderful sniper fire wouldn't just be gone—it would be replaced with

Judicators targeting *them*. Man, did she miss Mills. He'd have loved this firefight.

"Let's move," the captain bellowed, charging into the room from the north corridor. He layered a series of well-placed blasts into the unsuspecting Judicators, downing three before they were even aware of the new threat.

Lena came in next, taking out a Judicator herself. She paused to help the most ancient Primo that Hannan had ever seen. Behind them came a familiar black man with chrome eyes. He carried a limp female figure, her long dark hair trailing along the ground as the big man hurried behind Nolan. Hannan recognized both of them from the station where they'd ambushed the captain, and still remembered slamming a pipe into the black man's face. She wanted to ask why they were suddenly working together, but knew Nolan didn't have time to explain. If the captain trusted them, she had to as well.

"Now, Edwards!" Hannan roared.

Edwards lurched from cover, limping into an awkward run. Hannan popped from cover, as did Annie. Both picked their targets carefully, looking for Judicators trying to stop Edwards. Captain Nolan quickly figured out what they were doing, adding his own fire as he sprinted toward the south corridor.

Plasma began raining from above, and Hannan ducked to the right as a shot cratered the floor where she'd been about to step. She rolled behind a table, her rifle tumbling across the floor, out of reach.

"Screw it," Hannan said. She charged forward, snatching the rifle as she passed. Plasma balls rained down around her, but—miraculously—none hit. She zig-zagged through the wreckage littering the library floor, vaulting the remains of a table to catch up to the others.

Edwards shoulder-checked another Judicator, knocking it from his path. Then he backhanded another, sending it spinning into the wall. Annie and Nolan were cutting down targets with precision, so Hannan started directing her fire behind them. More and more Judicators were closing, and she did her best to discourage them.

They reached the safety of the corridor, sprinting head-long down the corridor. Edwards shrunk against the wall, letting everyone pass.

"What are you doing, Private?" she asked, darting back to Edwards.

"I'm going to slow them down, sir," Edwards said, resolved.

"Screw that," Hannan said, slapping his leg. It was hot to the touch. "Move your ass, Private. We don't need a heroic last stand. We need to get the hell off this station."

Then Hannan turned and ran. Edwards followed, something grinding in his leg with every clattering step. Bursts of plasma followed them, more than one striking Edwards in the back. He stumbled, but kept moving.

Ahead of them, Nolan stood next to the airlock door, beckoning them forward. "Go, go!"

Hannan redoubled her speed, sprinting like she'd never done in her life. She dove into the airlock, landing between Lena and the ancient Primo. Edwards hurried in after her. Plasma splashed the walls next to the door as Nolan pounded the airlock control. Two more plasma bursts shot through, scoring the walls, as the door inched closed behind them, cutting off pursuit.

44

PRIDELESS

Fizgig clenched and unclenched her claws, staring at the starmap on the *Claw*'s view screen. Many vessels were still breaking orbit and diving for the sun.

"What will you do, Mighty Fizgig?" Khar's voice rumbled behind her. Fizgig didn't turn to face him. She couldn't, not yet. Mow had orchestrated the situation masterfully, and for the first time in her life Fizgig felt powerless.

She studied the vessels moving toward the Helios Gate. Every last Leonis Pride vessel was departing after Mow, headed to war against the humans. A smattering of privateers and merchant vessels were all that remained, the dregs of the Tigris. The prideless.

Her tail rose a bit, and her shoulders squared. There just might be a way. "Tell me, Khar, what is your lifedream?"

Khar eyed her quizzically, whiskers twitching as he seemed to consider the question. His words were more deliberate than she'd heard him use before. "I wish to find a pride, Mighty Fizgig. I have long hoped that would be among the Leonis, as that is your pride."

"Izzy, what of you? What is your lifedream?" Fizgig asked, watching the snowy cat as she considered. Izzy's eyes were large and lent her a deceptive innocence, one particularly effective on the humans.

"Khar has spoken it, Mighty Fizgig. I wish to find a home, to be a part of a pride. Your pride." Izzy's ears were fully erect, her eyes even wider than usual as she awaited Fizgig's reply.

Fizgig considered both answers for long moments, her tail swishing lazily behind her. This would be a bold move, one that no one would expect. Mow assumed her removed as a threat, but she was about to show him exactly how mistaken he'd been. It meant breaking tradition, but there was no law forbidding it. Just because it hadn't been done in over a century didn't mean she couldn't do it.

"Izzy, open a channel to the entire system," Fizgig ordered, moving to sit on her chair. She straightened her cushions, forcing herself to affect a grace and poise she didn't feel.

"We are connected, Mighty Fizgig," Izzy said, nodding demurely.

"Mighty Tigris, hear me," she boomed, her voice filling the bridge of the *Claw*. "All know who I am. Fizgig Mankiller, Fizgig the Scourge, Fizgig Swift-Death. I have lived my life among Leonis Pride, for they were the strongest. Today, Mow proved that is no longer the case, and for the first time I am ashamed to be Leonis.

"So I have decided that I am Leonis no longer. I renounce my name. I am Fizgig Prideless." Fizgig rose from her chair and stared directly into the screen. "Today I build a new pride: Pride Fizgig. Any Tigris who stands with me will have a home in this pride. All are welcome, no matter your lineage, or past glory. Stand with me, and we'll show the Leonis what strength is."

Then Fizgig made a slashing motion, and Izzy terminated the feed.

Fizgig took a deep breath, tail flicking behind her as she stalked back to her chair. Would they come? Was she right about the lifedream of nearly every prideless?

Several moments passed. Khar eyed her silently, more introspective than he'd been when he'd served under her. It was a welcome change, a sign of his growing maturity. That would be important in the days ahead. He was the one most likely to succeed her, though Izzy was another possibility, even if she couldn't yet see it in herself.

"Sir, we're being hailed. By several vessels," Izzy said, glancing at Fizgig, then back at her console. "Over a dozen vessels have hailed us. Nineteen. Make that twenty-two."

"Open a channel to every vessel that hailed us," Fizgig said, giving her pillow one last fluff before settling into her most regal pose. She waited until Izzy nodded before speaking. "Your boldness is rewarded. You are prideless no longer. Now, we go to war, to teach our enemies the meaning of fear. Not against the humans, but against Mow."

She turned to Izzy, making another slashing gesture. Fizgig didn't speak until the view screen had returned to a star field. "Pick the four smallest vessels, and dispatch them to the other prides. They must be told what's happening with our home world."

45

BAD NEWS

Dryker imagined that most of the captains among the 14th were more than a little nervous. He would have been, in their place. Seven Primo carriers moving into their ranks was just a tad threatening, especially when a single carrier could handily wipe out the entire 14th. Dryker would probably have wet his pants when the drones started flowing out of the carriers. Normally those drones meant swift death. They swarmed the human vessels, but instead of attacking, each drone extended a mass of long, spindly arms.

"I sure hope you know what you're doing." Sheng's voice came over the comm. "We could all be space debris in seconds if the Primo get testy."

"Just sit tight and enjoy the free service," Dryker replied, watching as drones began towing cannons to each vessel. Little specks of blue began appearing at the end of each drone's arm—some sort of torch, Dryker imagined. The idea that attack drones could also effect repairs was mind-boggling. It made them far more versatile than he'd have guessed, and uncovered another layer of Primo technical superiority.

Dryker's comm buzzed. He fished it out, realizing it was Fizgig calling. Dryker looked around. Celendra and her guards were within earshot, but no one else. Dryker tapped the *Accept* button. "Glad to see you're still kicking. What have you got to report?"

"Catastrophe," Fizgig hissed. Dryker had never seen her so agitated, not even when she still believed he'd blown up one of their science vessels. "Your fleets have attacked Tigrana itself."

"That's suicide. There's no way we could breach your defenses," Dryker said, utterly confused.

"Normally that would be true," Fizgig said. She paused. "What I tell you would be considered treason, but I trust that you will not take advantage of this fact. Mow has moved the orbital defense platforms. He has stripped the fleets. Our world is unprotected, save for a few privateers."

"Oh my God," Dryker said, nearly dropping the comm. "Mow and Mendez must have worked together to arrange this. Do you have any idea what's going on with the battle?"

"Not yet," Fizgig said, sighing. "I have gathered the few troops I can, and am going there now to try to stop Mow. I do not know what you can do to convince the humans to stand down, but whatever it is...do it. You do not understand the depth of hatred that attacking our world will cause."

Dryker disagreed silently. He knew exactly what effect attacking Tigrana would have—and that, if they didn't stop it, the Void Wraith had all but won the war.

46

INTERROGATION

Nolan took a deep breath before entering their makeshift brig. He wasn't looking forward to this part, but he needed answers, and quickly. Lena and Atrea were hard at work sifting through the data they'd found, though Atrea was inconsolable about the loss of the master cube. Even if the Void Wraith left the library intact—and they wouldn't—it meant that priceless knowledge had been lost forever. Nolan was no scholar, but even he felt the impact.

Hannan and Annie were enjoying some well deserved rack time. Only Edwards was unoccupied, so Nolan had set him to watch the prisoners. Edwards was still missing an arm, but several tiny blue drones worked continuously on the other battle damage. They swarmed around him like flies on a rhino.

Nolan stepped into the 'brig,' an area of the Void Wraith ship that had been used to harvest humans. It involved large, clear tanks, usually full of an amber liquid. The tanks were strong enough to withstand plasma fire from Edwards, which made them perfect to use as cells.

Nolan strode down the row of tanks, stopping in front of the last two. Delta stood in one, metal arms crossed as he stared impassively at Nolan. The other tank held Kathryn, whose expression couldn't have been more the opposite of Delta's. She wore her emotions openly: pain and regret mingled with guilt. He'd seen them before, and suspected they were there to appeal to his softer side.

Kathryn was canny enough to know that the only card she could play was Nolan's feelings. Her OFI training would allow nothing else.

Nolan couldn't afford to be caught in that trap, so he hadn't even spoken to her yet. He wouldn't, not until he felt ready to deal with her.

"Edwards, open Delta's tank about six inches," Nolan said, nodding to Edwards.

The private raised his remaining arm, pressing it against the terminal. A moment later Delta's tank cracked open with a hiss. A small gap appeared, not enough to slip through, but enough to speak.

"Hello, Delta," Nolan said, nodding. He rested his hand on his sidearm, careful to keep out of arm's reach.

"Hello, Nolan," Delta said, returning the nod. "This is the first interrogation, I take it? Standard OFI? Get the baseline, to give you something to compare future interrogations against?"

"That's the general idea, yes," Nolan said, smiling grimly. He knew Delta had been in the UFC, but beyond a brief dossier he didn't know much about the man's life before he'd been...changed. Once upon a time, Delta had been Captain Edison, with a redacted file dating back at least a decade.

"You're deviating from protocol," Delta said, scratching at the corner of his eye, where chrome and skin met.

"Shouldn't you have at least one other officer here to observe?"

"Probably. I'm not a part of OFI, or even the UFC any more," Nolan said, shifting his weight to his other foot. He should have brought down a chair. "We're not here to talk about me, though. We're here to talk about you. Why don't we start with why you chose to betray your employers?"

"You remember the first time we met, back on Coronas 6?" Delta asked, face as impassive as ever.

"Yes."

"When you captured me, I told you a bit about the chip they were using to control me." Delta winced, raising a hand to his temple. After a long pause, he continued. "That chip is still in my head. It's a behavioral modification chip. I do what it wants, and I get rewarded with pleasure. I don't do what it wants, and it makes me crave death. Just talking about it gives me the worst—"

Delta's hand shot out, and Nolan took an instinctive step back. His weapon was out of its holster, aimed at Delta. Delta wasn't paying attention, though; he'd braced himself against the wall of the tank. His teeth were gritted, and a sheen of sweat dotted his forehead now.

Nolan had seen pain before, and this was some of the worst. He waited until Delta's breathing had slowed a little before speaking. "So you've been coerced into helping Reid, you saw an opportunity to get free, and you took it?" he asked, keeping his tone neutral.

It sounded a little too convenient, but if Delta had wanted to harm Nolan, all he'd have had to do was let Kathryn take him. If this was a deception, Nolan had no idea what the motive was.

"That's the gist of it, yeah," Delta said. He'd gone a shade paler, but was composing himself. "I'm hoping you can use all this Void Wraith tech to get the chip out. In exchange, I can offer two things."

"What would those be?" Nolan asked, glancing at Kathryn's cell. She stared at Nolan, head cocked as if trying to puzzle out the conversation even though she couldn't hear it.

"First, if you can deactivate my chip, you can deactivate it in others. At least a quarter of the senior officers in the UFC are now chipped," Delta explained. "More and more captains are brought into the fold every day, all answering to Mendez. He's training them like dogs, breaking them so they'll do what they're told. You want to stop Mendez and get humanity fighting the right enemy? It starts with deactivating my chip."

"Okay," Nolan said, nodding. He definitely agreed with Delta's assessment about the chip being the top priority. "What's the second thing?"

"I can tell you about the *thing* they put in her," Delta said, nodding toward Kathryn. "I can also tell you who, or rather *what*, she works for. Be ready, though. This shit is going to give you nightmares."

REAL CREEPY SHIT

Nolan walked over to the brig's wall, set his back to it, and slid to a sitting position. He stared at Delta, struggling to comprehend the story he'd just been told. It was outlandish, more than a little terrifying...and absolutely plausible, given everything they knew.

"Tell it to me one more time," Nolan said, resting his hands in his lap. "I want to make sure I didn't miss anything."

"Yeah," Edwards said, his heavy metal frame scraping across the floor as he crept a little closer to Delta's vat-cell. "Tell us about the Eye. That's some real creepy shit, right there."

"All right," Delta said, calmly. He folded his arms, and they clinked when he did so. "I know this is a lot to take in. I'll hit the highlights again. There's a giant floating eye in the Jakaren system, near something Reid called a supermassive black hole. This thing is alive. It gets in your head; I could feel it slithering through mine. All sorts of ships were there to feed the Eye, and I'm positive I don't want to know what it does with the people being dropped off on the surface."

Delta shook his head, paling. He cleared his throat, then continued.

"Anyway, this Eye creates these larvae, like a bunch of little tadpoles—or maybe leeches. It turned out that was why we'd gone there, to pick up a load. They use these things to subvert people, and Reid left with an entire canister. Hundreds of these things."

"And one of them is inside Kathryn?" Nolan asked, shifting his attention to Kathryn's vat. At some point she'd also gotten tired of standing, and now sat cross-legged in the center of her cell. Her face had gone impassive; all attempts to appeal to his emotions were gone.

"I'm afraid so," Delta said, also looking at Kathryn. "If you've got a way to get it out of her, I'd do it quick. You remember when I was first running with Reid, before you and your girlfriend caught me? He's deteriorated a lot since then. I'm betting whatever that parasite is, it kills the host eventually."

"Lovely," Nolan said, rising restlessly. "Ship, have you been monitoring this conversation?"

"I have," Ship responded.

"Is there a way to scan Kathryn? To identify this parasite somehow?" Nolan asked, looking up. Ship wasn't any*where*, so looking up didn't make a lot of sense, but he couldn't help but imagine she was above him somewhere. There. He'd called Ship *she*. When had that happened?

"I believe so," Ship responded. "I can have a scan prepared. It will take time to calibrate the scan, otherwise the burst of radiation would kill the prisoner."

"Make doubly sure the test is safe before you administer it," Nolan said, then corrected himself. "In fact, contact me when the test is ready. I want to be here when you administer it."

"Acknowledged, Captain," Ship said, cheerfully.

Nolan turned back to Delta. "Now let's deal with the problem we *can* attack. Ship, can you use this scan, or a related sensor, to trigger some sort of EMP inside the vat?"

"I believe so. If we modulate the burst correctly, it will deliver a concentrated EMP, without much of the accompanying radiation. However, it is still possible that the subject may experience inadvisably high levels," Ship cautioned.

"Do it," Delta said, mouth firming into a line.

"All right," Nolan said, rising to his feet. He approached the vat. "Edwards, close the cell."

Edwards scraped his way back to the console, and the opening in the vat closed. Nolan met Delta's gaze, raising a questioning eyebrow. Delta nodded.

"Administer the pulse, Ship," Nolan commanded. He braced himself, but nothing visible happened. No sudden flash of light, or explosion of sound. Nothing.

"The pulse has been administered," Ship said.

"Open the cell six inches again, Edwards," Nolan ordered.

The cell slid open. Delta stood, panting, one hand planted against the glass. He stared off into space with those chromed eyes.

"I can't see," he said, his eyes roaming as he looked around.

"The EMP probably shorted your eyes," Nolan suggested. "We'll have the ship take a look in the Judicator assembly area. Do you feel any different?"

"I'll find out," Delta said, sinking to his knees. He braced himself against the glass, as if he expected to fall. "My name is...Carl Edison."

Then Delta began to sob. His body was wracked with them, and he huddled down into a fetal position. Nolan approached the glass, heartfelt pity for the man overpowering everything else. They'd been enemies, but not by choice.

"We'll pay them back for this, I promise you," Nolan offered.

The words had a profound effect. Delta stopped sobbing. He uncoiled, rising slowly back to his feet, and facing the gap in the glass with those unseeing eyes. "We'll get them back all right. I'm going to kill Reid, and then I'm going to end Mendez. They'll never do this to anyone, not ever again."

48

THE FORGE

Lena chewed the end of her stylus, aware that the poor thing was scored with teeth marks. It was a guilty habit she'd picked up at the Academy on Tigrana, and she did it unconsciously when reading. Fortunately, she stocked a lot of extra styluses for just that reason. She fished a fresh one from her satchel, turning back to her sketch.

"Which story are you reading, little sister?" Atrea asked, peering over at the drawing. "What an odd image. What are you doodling?"

"This is my interpretation of the Forge," Lena said, eyeing her work critically. The artful curves made the vessel look similar to modern Primo vessels, but she'd made it larger, and given it a number of weapons.

"The Forge," Atrea said, leaning forward in her chair. "That's an old story. One of the oldest. You think you've found something significant there?"

"Possibly," Lena said, uncertainly. She found the older Primo scholar intimidating, and felt like a prideless next to a Leonis matriarch. "I have a theory, anyway."

"Let's hear it," Atrea said, waving a hand over her tablet. The screen went dark. "I'm sure whatever you're about to say is more interesting than Miffar's interpretation of the Void Wraith 'myth.'"

"Well," Lena began, curling her tail in her lap. She took it in both hands, speaking slowly. "The myth says that the Elder Gods did battle with the Void Wraith. I can't find many references to these Elder Gods, but those stories that do reference them claim that they gave birth to the Primo. That certainly sounds like an earlier group. It's possible that these Elder Gods are the first Primo empire, and that this tells the tale of the first war with the Void Wraith. If that's the case, it sounds like the Void Wraith were defeated by the Forge."

"That's a logical interpretation," Atrea said, giving a tiny smile. "If you are correct, that might mean that the Forge was a real vessel, and if so it might be one we could still locate."

"That's it exactly," Lena said excitedly. "The myth says the ship returned to the Birthplace. If I'm right, that Birthplace corresponds to a celestial body somewhere. Maybe the original Primo home world?"

"Quite possibly," Atrea said, bobbing her head. "I know of a number of potential sources of information on the Birthplace, but all are among our most ancient lore. I do not know if we salvaged enough to provide the actual location."

"I have an idea there," Lena said. She spoke to the air around her. "Ship, can you hear me?"

"Affirmative, Lena of Pride Leonis," Ship said, cheerfully.

"I'd like you to reference all mythology you have access to, and have it sent to this terminal," Lena commanded, grinning at Atrea. The scholarly woman hadn't made the connection yet, but she would.

"You can't mean..." Atrea said, her tiny mouth falling open into a comically small O. "You possess a data cube from the second Primo empire?"

"We do," Lena said, grinning. Her tail writhed anxiously in her grip. "This VI doesn't contain an entire archive, but its knowledge is considerable. Since the second empire wasn't as far removed, they may have clearer information about this Forge."

49

INTO THE FRAY

"Sir, the *Veracruz* is reporting drive issues," Juliard called. She sat at the makeshift CIC station Dryker had had assembled the previous day. Now that he was running a human fleet in addition to the Primo, he needed the instrumentation necessary to command them.

"Tell them we're moving out in ten minutes. If they can't get the problem isolated they're to effect repairs, and get there as soon as possible," Dryker instructed, shifting uncomfortably on the Primo throne.

He'd considered taking one of the few capital ships from the 14th as his flagship, but had ultimately decided it would be better to stay aboard the *First Light*. Being aboard a destroyer again would be wonderful, but it wouldn't do much for cohesion between the two races.

"Sir, the *Orion* is on the line," Juliard said.

Dryker connected his comm, audio only. "This is *First Light* actual; go ahead, *Orion*."

"Sir, if the *Veracruz* stays behind, we're losing our only battleship," Sheng said. "The *Orion* is a frigate. We could have our generator moved to the *Veracruz* in under an hour, if *Veracruz* gives us a little more manpower."

"You're willing to sit this one out?" Dryker asked, more than a little surprised. Sheng had a bloodthirsty reputation, which was why she'd ended up in the 14th.

"No, sir. I figure my crew can be distributed to other vessels. I also think you need a first officer," Sheng said, bluntly.

"All right, I'll notify the *Orion*. Have your drive wired up to the new Primo weaponry. Their main core can handle normal ship functions, which should remove enough of the load for it to work," Dryker said, musing aloud. He turned to Juliard. "Have Sheng brought aboard and get that drive shuffled, Lieutenant."

Juliard bent to her station with a nod, and Dryker enjoyed a full twenty seconds of silence before Celendra spoke. "Admiral, I've received word that all Primo are in place. There is some hesitation about having our people aboard your ships, but I have reassured them that we will not be treated as expendable."

That last was part question, and Dryker knew she was looking for reassurance. He wasn't good at this crap, but he did his best. "Let them know that we'll keep them out of direct combat. All they need to do is ensure their weapons keep working. That's the only possible way we're going to be able to reach Mendez." Turning to Juliard, he asked, "Lieutenant, have we heard from the *Essels* yet?"

"Negative, sir," Juliard said, then corrected herself a moment later. "Strike that. They're entering the photosphere now. Captain Ygris is hailing us."

"On screen," Dryker said, forgetting there was no screen on the *First Light*.

Celendra waved a hand, and a portion of the dome

shifted to show Ygris's grizzled face. The man looked like he'd been through a wood chipper, scars criss-crossing both cheeks. "I've got that data you wanted, sir. Broadcasting it now."

"Give me the short version," Dryker said, stepping from the throne and approaching the part of the dome where Celendra was displaying the captain's face.

"The 5th, 11th, and 4th are already here," Ygris explained. "They're in a defensive position, orbiting Tigrana. Sir...it's bad. They conducted a sustained orbital bombardment. The entire southern continent is gone, sir."

"And the Tigris forces?" Dryker asked, stifling the hot surge in his belly. Were they too late?

"It looks like the entire Leonis Pride is moving to engage. At least seventy ships, sir," Ygris said, scrubbing thick fingers through his bristly hair. "I'd lay odds on the Tigris. They're pissed off, and even if they're a little outnumbered, they're fighting for their homes."

Ygris was right. If the battle played out, both sides would be savaged so badly they'd never recover. They had to stop this. Had to.

50

BEGIN THE ASSAULT

Fizgig strode through the halls of her ship, shoulders squared and tail held high. The ship would never recover, and entire sections were open to space. Yet she still flew, and Fizgig was proud of her. The *Claw* had a soul of her own, and that soul would never give up. No matter the odds.

Fizgig made her way deeper into the ship, the whir of power tools and the shouts of techs coming from up ahead. She strode purposefully onto the deck, pausing to survey the fighter bay. The handful of remaining darts had been gathered into the area closest to the functional launch tube. The few racks of ordinance were stacked near them. There were precious few of either, but at least her crew had been replenished.

They stood in neat, even ranks. The only notable exception was the techs, and even they paused in their work. Every last pair of eyes was on her. She stared back, proud and a little sad. These people had been marginalized for so long that they were willing to risk everything just to earn something she'd taken for granted her whole life: a name.

"Mighty Fizgig," the crowd chorused, nearly three hundred Tigris throats booming together. Every last soldier snapped to attention, and if there were a few stragglers, at least they'd made the attempt.

Fizgig stalked forward, prowling back and forth in front of the crowd. She studied them in silence for long moments before finally speaking. "We are Fizgig Pride. We are family. The first thing your family will teach you is honor. You are the equal of any Leonis. Remember that, and hold your head high."

More than one soldier straightened at that, and most adopted proud expressions. For many, it was the first time they'd been acknowledged by an officer, let alone a Pride leader. The ember of pride that had taken hold in each was delicate, and would need to be stoked, until it became a raging inferno. The way to achieve that was simple: victory.

"Our plan is simple, but devastatingly effective. We will allow the Leonis to engage the humans." She stopped pacing and raised her Primo rifle to her chest, displaying it proudly. "Admiral Mow will lead from the rear, like the coward he is. We will ambush him, and wrest the fate of our people from his bloody corpse."

She stabbed the pistol up into the air, firing a blast at the ceiling. Answering blasts rippled through the crowd, mostly slug-throwing weapons, stolen or purchased from humans. Eventually Fizgig raised a paw, waiting three seconds for silence. Most fell into line, but a few still fired and laughed.

"Silence!" Fizgig roared, cutting off the stragglers. "Today you will learn discipline, the coin with which you will purchase greatness. Act like warriors. Dismissed."

Fizgig turned on her heel, stalking from the barracks and into the *Claw's* aft corridor. She circled around to the top of the ship, taking the only remaining route to the bridge. The *Claw* was just as bedraggled as Fizgig's new pride.

That didn't deter her. If anything, it seemed fitting. She was old, and she was weary. So, too, was the *Claw* old and weary. Both should have returned to the home world long since, to foster the next generation of kits while waiting for Tigrana's embrace.

Fizgig took her time reaching the bridge, using the time to visualize Mow. She pictured her paws around his throat, saw herself biting down savagely and ending his life. That had always been the way of it for her, seeing the kill before she made it. It gave her a certainly, a knowing of sorts. She knew Mow would die, and that she'd be the one that took his life.

51

SCAN

Nolan suppressed his agitation as Kathryn's tube filled with pink light. Lena manned a terminal near Edwards, bent almost double to scan some sort of readings. Kathryn gave no outward sign of discomfort, peering curiously at the light surrounding her. Of course, no outward sign didn't mean much. If Lena or the ship had misjudged the proper amount of radiation, Kathryn would die within days.

"Nolan," Lena said, finally straightening from the panel. She clasped her tail in both paws. "The test will take roughly two minutes. During that time, there is something you need to know. Atrea and I debated telling you, as we aren't positive, but we think we've found something important."

"Something that could help us?" Nolan said, perking up slightly. They desperately needed a win at this point.

"During the original Primo empire, they utilized something called the Forge. Sometimes this is referred to as a place, other times as a weapon. It's unclear precisely what it is, but several myths from the second Primo empire suggest it was a vessel," Lena explained, blinking those feline eyes. "If I am correct, that vessel was never destroyed. The myths say that it was returned to the Birthplace."

"And you think this Forge could help us against the Void Wraith?" Nolan asked, intensely curious. "And that it's still around, even after so many thousands of years?"

"Yes, and yes," Lena said, nodding. "The Primo built the Forge after they were first attacked by the Void Wraith. They used it to create the technology that later became their ships and weapons. The Forge was part research vessel, part weapon. By itself, the ship would be incredibly formidable, but it likely contains technological secrets beyond even the Primo's most advanced levels."

The implications were staggering. Nolan suddenly understood one of the possible motives this Eye might have. Assuming it was overseeing the creation of an army in the Milky Way, it would be just as interested in the Forge as they were. Nolan couldn't be certain, but this certainly seemed like a reason to blow up the Primo libraries. If a ship like that existed, you'd definitely want to prevent your enemies from finding out about it.

"You said it returned to the Birthplace?" Nolan asked, his excitement mounting.

"I did," Lena replied, ears drooping. "Atrea and I have no idea where the Birthplace is, not yet anyway. We'll continue to study, but some of the data we needed was destroyed back at the library."

Nolan stifled a surge of frustration. Just when he'd thought they might have a leg up. There was nothing for it, though. They had to fight with the weapons at hand. If they managed to end the war between humans and Tigris, maybe then they could find this ship.

The console behind Lena began beeping. She turned to

face it, raising a hand to her mouth. "Oh, my. Nolan, you need to see this."

Nolan hurried over, bending to study the data Lena was looking at. It showed a mass of red tendrils spiraling through Kathryn's body, a thin latticework that traced the nervous system and led to a thick mass centered around the base of the spine.

"Can we remove it?" Nolan asked.

Lena shook her head sadly. "This is way beyond my capabilities," she said. "Our best neurosurgeons would be hard-pressed to do anything. This thing has effectively merged with her nervous system. I have no idea how we'd kill it without killing her."

"All right," Nolan said, taking a deep breath. There had to be a way to fix this, not just for Kathryn's sake.

Though, he had to admit, it was mostly for her sake.

"There's more bad news," Lena said, swiping the screen until it showed another graph. "That's the rate of advance. This thing is taking over more and more of her body. If the process continues, I'd guess she has no more than six to eight weeks before it kills her."

As terrible as it was, Nolan didn't give in to it. They had a job to do. He couldn't help her, but he'd already helped Delta, and could help countless others.

THE PLAN

"So that's the story," Nolan explained, resting his hands on the conference room's chrome table. "We need a way to disable the chips, something wide-scale enough to affect them all at the same time. We're some of the best and brightest out there. Suggestions?"

Lena and Atrea looked at each other, as if each was unsure who should defer. Nolan caught Hannan hiding a smile out of the corner of his eye, clearly amused by the scholars as they tripped over each other trying to be polite.

"I believe we may have a way," Atrea said, resting a leathery hand on Lena's shoulder. "Lena, please correct me if you have a better approach, but we don't need to disable all the chips. We merely need to disable the transmitter. Who holds the leash? Eliminate that threat, and it won't matter if these men have chips. They're not dangerous if no one can activate them."

Nolan blinked at the simple audacity of the suggestion. It made sense. He held his tongue, waiting for the others to offer their opinions of Atrea's idea before he weighed in. That was a trick he'd picked up from Dryker.

"How will we find the transmitter?" Hannan asked, suddenly more interested in the conversation. "If it's Mendez, won't he just issue his orders before the battle? Delta, how often do you receive orders on that thing?"

"Almost never," Delta said, his words just above a whisper. He'd been mostly silent since Ship had used the Judicator assembly to restore his eyesight.

"Excellent point," Nolan said, drawing everyone's attention. "The only way we'd be able to find the transmitter is if we were able to bait the person in control into using it. Delta, what kind of circumstance might force them to use it?"

"Hmm," Delta said, rousing from his funk. "I'd guess one of two men will be holding the reins, either Admiral Mendez or Admiral Chu. Those are the top dogs among the human brass. One of those two men is likely to be in charge of the assault on Tigrana."

"It will be Chu," Nolan said, without hesitation. His eyes narrowed, as he considered his former benefactor. "Mendez is too smart to be caught in the open like that. Chu likes glory, so I'm betting Mendez puts him in charge of the battle. We find a way to force Chu to activate the chips, which identifies his flagship. Then we attack that ship."

"What if you're wrong about the person in charge?" Lena asked, sipping her tea as if she were drinking from fine porcelain instead of a military surplus cup.

"It won't matter," Nolan said. "Whoever uses the chip is in command, so if we get a signal we take down whoever is using it."

"We're down to a handful of Judicators, just the ones that were being repaired when we hit the library," Hannan cautioned. "Edwards is in a bad way, too. He needs a major refitting. Even if he didn't, he's not going to fit through a

UFC starship's corridors. That means it's the people in this room, plus a handful of expendable robots, to take on an entire capital ship. Their Marine detachment will be at least thirty-six men, and that's if it's been stripped. It's much more likely they'll have over a hundred battle-trained Marines."

"That's why they can't be allowed to see us coming. We're going to use Void Wraith cloaking tech," Nolan said. He couldn't help but grin as he pressed the button on the top of his new belt buckle. A tingle of static electricity rippled out from the belt, up to his head and down to his feet. A moment later, Hannan's jaw fell open. Nolan tapped the button again and the field dissipated. "We have four of these. That's enough to get a small infiltration team onto the bridge. They won't be ready for plasma fire, and they won't see us coming. We kill Chu, and take the chip transmitter."

"That still leaves the issue of the chipped soldiers," Delta cautioned. He seemed uncomfortable with everyone staring at him, but after clearing his throat he finally continued. "If they receive an order, they'll follow it. Even if we stop Chu, the captains will follow whatever order he gives. They'll take suicidal action, and if he tells them to ram the Tigris, they will."

Nolan considered that, waiting to see if anyone else spoke. No one did.

"We're going to have to jam the chip's quantum entanglement," Nolan finally said, the plan forming as he spoke. "We can get the entanglement from the chip in Delta, and when we hit the system we can start broadcasting. That will prevent the person from giving the order."

"How do we detect that person transmitting?" Atrea asked in her gravelly voice. She leaned forward, meeting Nolan's gaze. "If you jam the entanglement, then you block the very signal you're monitoring for."

"Good point," Nolan said, sighing. "I can't think of a way around that."

"Pardon me, Captain," Ship said. "I may be able to solve that problem."

"How?" Nolan asked, glancing up.

"I can write an algorithm that will monitor the entanglement. Any time it detects an activation, it will also activate," Ship explained. "This will log any attempt to use the network, and prevent the bulk of any message from arriving."

"Your algorithm wouldn't be detected until it started jamming, right?" Nolan asked, already warming to the plan.

"Precisely, Captain," Ship confirmed. "It would lay dormant until a signal was detected."

"Then I think we have a workable plan, people," Nolan said, rising to his feet. "Hannan, I want a detailed assault plan for a team to reach the bridge undetected. See what you and Annie can come up with. Lena, Atrea, keep working on this Forge."

"Captain, we're receiving an incoming transmission," Ship said.

"Put it on screen," Nolan said. A moment later, a hologram sprang into existence on the far side of the room. It showed a weary-looking Captain Dryker, still aboard the cavernous Primo vessel.

"Nolan, we've just arrived in-system at Tigrana. You need to get here. Now," Dryker said, expression pained. "The Tigris are beginning their assault on the human fleets. The 11th is bombarding the planet."

53

ORDERS

Mendez was tired. The joining had provided him with many abilities, but using them came with a cost. Every day, he added another layer of exhaustion, and he knew he couldn't keep this up forever. Sooner or later, he'd buckle under the strain. He suspected the larva knew that—counted on it, even. That was troubling, but there was nothing he could do about it. God knew he'd tried. Over and over, at first. Now he accepted his role.

"Connect me with Chu," Mendez ordered, withdrawing a cigar from the breast pocket of his uniform. He took his time cutting the end, and then lighting it. By the time he'd taken his first puff, the view screen had flickered to life.

Chu's bridge was older than Mendez's ship, and the stations on Chu's vessel were still manned by active personnel. Mendez could see at a glance that they were terrified of Chu, and for good reason. He looked positively ghastly atop the captain's chair, his belly and limbs slightly distended. His skin was nearly translucent. If Mendez needed any proof that the larva meant ill for him, the proof was in Chu's health. How long had Chu been implanted before he'd done the same to Mendez? That would determine the timetable, the amount of time Mendez had before he looked just like Chu.

"What do you want, Mendez? The Tigris are about to launch their assault. I need to attend to the battle," Chu said, his eyes narrowing in distaste.

Mendez had grown used to the contempt, and could hardly blame Chu. Chu had been the one to recruit Mendez, and before that had been the top agent among the admiralty. Now that was Mendez, and Chu had no one but himself to blame.

"That's why I'm contacting you, actually," Mendez said, giving Chu a friendly smile. "I wanted to clarify how this battle is to be conducted. I'm broadcasting a series of deployment orders now."

Chu glanced down at his data pad, his scowl deepening as he read. After nearly a minute his eyes shot up, spearing Mendez. "I can't give these orders. Some of these are suicidal. This is career ending. I'll be stripped of rank, if we even survive."

"Regrettably," Mendez said, without an ounce of regret, "the masters have decided that such a sacrifice is necessary. You'll send the best unimplanted captains to their deaths. The Tigris are receiving similar orders. Those likely to oppose us, on both sides, need to die in this battle. Casualties need to be immense. Is that understood, Admiral Chu?"

Chu's face twisted in emotional agony. He wrestled with it, seemingly unable to speak. Mendez waited patiently, letting the man twist. He truly did regret losing an agent with Chu's influence, but the damage they'd inflict here made the sacrifice worth it. Today would mark the beginning of the end for all resistance to the masters.

In one fell swoop, they'd wipe out the strongest parts of

both humanity and the Tigris. After this, the implanted parts of their fleets would outnumber unimplanted parts. They could co-opt both species' militaries, using them to speed the masters' conquest. More, this attack ensured that the two races would never be able to unite.

"I understand," Chu finally said.

"Good. Best of luck, Admiral," Mendez said, then he severed the connection. He glanced at one of the drones jacked into the bridge. "Take us to the star's nadir point, then dive for the Helios Gate. I want to be gone by the time this battle gets underway."

54

CAREER SUICIDE

Chu wiped at his forehead, shocked when he saw the streak of red across the back of his hand. That wasn't sweat. It was blood. He began to tremble, struggling to hide from the truth he simply couldn't admit: the larva was still growing. As it grew, it fed on him. He was dying, sacrificed to the masters in a very literal way. He could feel it slithering through his nervous system, infecting every part of him like a cancer.

What terrified him the most was how much he welcomed it.

"Sir," one of his bridge techs called. He hadn't bothered to learn their names. "The Tigris fleet will intercept in sixty seconds. Do you have orders you wish to convey to the captains? Several have already hailed us."

"Yes," Chu said, straightening despite the pain that had crept from his back into his chest. "Have the *Defiant*, the *Equilibrium*, the *Sojourn*, the *Midway*, and the *Rebel* move to intercept. The 11th will continue their orbital bombardment. The rest of the fleet will stand by for additional orders."

The tech protested. "Sir, are you sure—"

"Relay those orders, Lieutenant," Chu said, silencing the lieutenant with a chopping gesture.

"Aye, sir," the lieutenant said, moving back to his console.

Chu understood the man's protest. By continuing the bombardment, they would weaken their defense and drive the Tigris into a suicidal frenzy. The Tigris would stop at nothing to destroy the 11th fleet, the one that had belonged to Admiral Kelley until recently. It was the single largest concentration of loyal officers in the fleet, and if the Tigris wiped them out it would break the back of UFC resistance.

Chu watched as the vessels he'd named drifted from the rest of the fleet. They moved out alone, five ships against seventy. Would this be the order that convinced the chipped captains to mutiny? It might be. Were Chu the man he'd been before the larva, he'd certainly have defied these orders.

Chu's hand drifted to the little black box in his pocket, which reassured him. If the chipped captains rebelled, at least he possessed the means of bringing them back into line. They'd do their duty, killing loyal Tigris and humans alike. When the dust settled, Chu would be dead, but the masters' plan would be that much closer to completion.

Chu was racked by a fit of coughing, and raised his hand to see specks of blood all over his palm. It wouldn't be long now. His only regret was that he wouldn't be around to savor that victory, or to see what hatched from his corpse.

55

BREAKING THE ACCORDS

A ragged mixture of human and Primo vessels emerged from the star's corona, moving far enough away to escape the worst of the magnetic fields. That would allow them to scan the rest of the system, and allow Dryker to get a feel for the disposition of the assembled fleets before he engaged. He watched as the dome flickered briefly, then icons began to appear.

Dryker stood resolute, watching the single most horrifying event he'd ever witnessed play out before him. The 11th fleet continued to bombard the surface, little streaks dropping from each vessel. Moments later mushroom clouds dotted the surface. Then more streaks, and more clouds. Most of the planet's southern continent was coated in dust and ash.

"Our records indicate that the southern continent was the most densely populated," Celendra said, shifting her weight as she stared at the planet. "Rarely have we seen an atrocity on this level. Were there no Void Wraith threat, if the Tigris petitioned us to wipe out humanity, I believe my people would do it."

"I'm not sure they'd be wrong to," Dryker said, deeply disturbed by what he was witnessing.

A mass of Tigris ships had been automatically tagged with blue triangles. The moment they registered, the human vessels became orange squares. Five squares broke from the main human fleet, moving to intercept. Nearly seventy triangles overwhelmed those squares. The move puzzled Dryker for a split second, until he remembered that the whole goal of this attack was to wipe out loyal human captains.

This needed to be stopped, as quickly as possible. The longer the battle went on, the more vessels on both sides would be destroyed. But how did you stop a war between races who had every reason to hate each other, races with a history of violent conflict?

He had to try.

"Celendra, can you broadcast me across the Quantum Network to all human vessels in system?" Dryker asked.

"Yes, give me a moment to establish the connection," Celendra said, touching a button on the bracelet on her wrist. Her skin was lighter than it had been the day before, more sky blue than sea foam. Was that typical for Primo? "There. You are live, Admiral."

"Attention, officers of the UFC," Dryker began, licking his lips, then plunging forward. "Three months ago, a battle took place in the Ghantan system. Humans and Tigris worked to stop a common threat. The people behind that threat twisted what happened there to convince our races to go to war. The Tigris are not our real enemy. Right now, each of you is receiving proof to back up my claims. Footage from battles with the Void Wraith, and evidence that the admiralty has been infiltrated.

"I know this is a big ask, but if we expect our race to

survive I need you to listen," Dryker said, wishing he could see the faces of the captains listening. Were they? "You can see that I'm surrounded by a Primo fleet. Most of the Primo have been wiped out, but the few remaining are willing to help us against a common enemy. Every vessel we lose today weakens us for the war to come.

"So I call on you to join me. Stop fighting the senseless war with the Tigris. For the love of God, stop bombarding their planet. You're breaking the accords," Dryker said, his voice cracking. "We're giving them every reason to hate us. Is that what we've become? Do you really believe it's okay to bomb women and children? Stop being used. Save your race. Or die senselessly, helping your enemies."

Dryker stopped talking, and a moment later Celendra tapped her bracelet. She turned slowly, hesitantly, to face him. "Do you think they will listen?"

"I don't know," Dryker said. "We're trained to follow orders, even orders we don't understand. But the evidence I broadcast will make a lot of the captains think. I wished we'd gotten here several hours ago. Now that combat has begun, it will be more difficult to convince them to pull away from it."

Dryker watched as the Tigris finished savaging the five vessels that had moved to engage them. They were now moving to circle the rest of the human fleet, to engage the 11th. The smart tactical decision would have been to have the 11th break off to engage, while the rest of the fleet flanked the Tigris.

Instead, the 11th continued their bombardment. The rest of the fleet sat there, clustered away from where they could protect the 11th. It presented the 11th's belly to an enemy already whipped into a frenzy. So Dryker tried again.

"Captains of the 11th, this time I'm speaking directly to

you. You can see the Tigris closing with you. Cease your bombardment, and retreat to take shelter with my fleet. I've got the bulk of the 14th, and half a dozen Primo warships," Dryker explained. "If you aren't willing to stop because of your conscience, do it for your survival. You are about to be wiped out to a man. For what?"

Dryker trailed off. Now all he could do was wait.

56

ASSESSMENT

Nolan toweled off, pulling on his uniform as quickly as he could. If the only thing Annie ever did was install showers, she'd have more than earned her keep. Dear God, he loved that woman.

He was jittery and exhausted, the result of prolonged stim use. He needed real sleep, but that wasn't happening today. Nolan buckled on his stealth belt, tucking his plasma pistol into the holster Annie had modified for him. He was continually impressed by her ability to improvise. She claimed the "underfunded 14th" was spoiled, and infantry would kill to have the castoffs the 14th disparaged. After seeing her handiwork Nolan had more respect for his ground-bound servicemen cousins.

He clipped the bracelet around his wrist, knowing he'd need his plasma blade on the way to the bridge of Chu's vessel. The blade was a much quieter method of killing, and stealth would be key as they infiltrated his ship. He was far from a master in its use, but given his success against Kathryn and her cyber Marines, he felt confident he could hold his own.

"Captain, the admiral has begun his speech," Hannan's voice crackled from the comm.

"Ship, broadcast Dryker's speech shipwide," Nolan ordered.

He listened as Dryker tried to convince the fleet captains to defect, and by the time the admiral was done Nolan was moving at a fast walk toward the bridge. Hannan and Annie were already there, but Atrea and Lena had closeted themselves down in the brig. They were studying the organism they'd found in Kathryn, trying to find a way to kill it without killing her. Since neither was good in a combat situation, he preferred they stick to a problem they might be able to solve.

"Captain," Delta said, striding onto the bridge. He seemed less hesitant than before. Maybe the few hours' nap had given him time to bury the intense emotion he was going through.

"We can't keep calling you 'Delta,'" Nolan said. He hadn't brought up the man's real name, because it seemed to pain the big Marine. "How do you want the crew to address you?"

Delta was silent for a moment, considering. When he finally spoke, it was on the heels of a grim smile. "'Delta' is just fine. They gave me the name as a curse, a way of breaking me, but they failed. So I'll take their name, and use it against them. I'm the weapon they made, and I'm going to do as much damage to them as possible. Besides, I can't just go back to being Edison. They've scrubbed that part of my life away. Whoever I am going forward, it isn't that same officer."

"Well said," Hannan offered, clapping Delta on the shoulder. "Everyone in the 14th is a little tarnished, and we've all got checkered pasts. You'll fit in great with this crew."

"And don't worry about your cybernetics," Edwards said from the corner. Most of his battle damage had been repaired, though his left arm was still missing. "I mean, I'm a frigging Judicator, right? You're, like, the fifth weirdest person on board. You totally belong here."

"Ship, are you standing by with that algorithm?" Nolan asked, watching the fleet dispositions change on the holographic display. Dryker had finished his speech, but in the two minutes since, not a single vessel had broken away to join him.

"Affirmative, Captain," Ship said. "I haven't detected any transmission using that quantum wavelength."

"Bring us closer to the massed human fleet," Nolan said, folding his arms. He was damned thankful for the Void Wraith cloaking tech. They could move freely throughout the battle, certain that their enemy was unaware of their presence. "Chu is there somewhere, on one of the capital ships. Probably one hanging back from the actual fighting. Let's get into position. He'll slip up, and the second he does, we engage."

57

CHU

"Sir, the Tigris have engaged the 11th," a tech said.

Chu ignored him, studying the view screen. The 11th had stopped their bombardment, and was shifting to engage the Tigris. They were outnumbered about three to one, and in a poor tactical position.

Tigris ships slammed into human vessels, devastating the entire outer line. The 11th began to buckle, ships trying to fall back without going into a full rout. Now was the time a good commander—the kind of commander he used to be—would step in.

"Have any of our ships responded to Dryker or broken away?" Chu asked, fingering the black box in his pocket. He'd use it if necessary, but would prefer to avoid that.

"No, sir," the lieutenant said. "Sir, the 11th is taking devastating losses. Are you sure you don't want to issue new orders?"

Chu drew his sidearm and shot the man in the face. The shocked officer collapsed bonelessly to the deck. A tiny plume of smoke rose from the barrel of Chu's pistol. He stared from bridge officer to bridge officer, but none was willing to meet his gaze. The survivors were all chipped, and they knew the kind of pain he could inflict.

"Who's trained to assume this fool's station?" Chu demanded.

Another lieutenant rushed forward, this one a short, redheaded woman in her early forties. She snapped a hasty salute, carefully averting her gaze. "I am, sir."

"Good, take over. And have someone clean up that mess," Chu demanded, returning to the captain's chair.

The 11th had shifted their formation, and the rear vessels had moved to reinforce their line. They were engaging the Tigris, who were starting to take casualties as well. The final outcome wasn't in question, but the move bought the surviving officers of the 11th some time. That wasn't a good thing, but there was little Chu could do, except withhold the the help they needed.

Pain stabbed through Chu's chest, black fingers settling around his heart. He could feel something slithering inside of him. Growing. Readying itself to emerge. It was a horrifying feeling, and part of his mind recognized that he should be doing everything possible to remove the parasite before it killed him.

The greater portion of his mind understood that this new being was superior to him in every way, and that giving his life to birth it was the only right, the only proper, course of action. He reached up to touch his cheek, and it came away bloody.

He needed to conclude this battle quickly.

58

APPEAL TO REASON

Dryker's heart broke as he watched the Tigris devastate the 11th fleet. Dozens of ships were burning, on both sides. The 11th was fighting back now, but they didn't have a prayer, not without assistance. Part of Dryker wanted to go to their aid, but attacking the Tigris would be playing right into the Void Wraith's hands. He needed to stop the combat, not escalate it.

"I have some idea of what you must have felt when the Void Wraith attacked Theras," Dryker said, taking a step closer to Celendra. The two might as well have been alone, as the dozens of interested Primo lined the back of the room. Not a single one spoke, each watching the battle with their expressions blank. Dryker knew there was some sort of tradition there, as this had the feeling of ritual. Damned if he knew what it meant, though.

"I believe you do," Celendra said, eyeing him sadly. A bead of milky sweat trickled down her forehead. "Would that there was an easy way to stop the fighting. Do you have another tactic?"

"I'm going to try one more time," Dryker said, nodding. "Go ahead and broadcast."

Celendra tapped her bracelet, then nodded to Dryker.

What the hell was he going to say that he hadn't already? What would convince the humans to break away?

The truth, that was what. Maybe that was the smartest way to flush him out, though. It might also convince some of the captains.

"Captains of the UFC, I'm going to try this one more time," Dryker said. "You can see the 11th being wiped out. Admiral Chu is standing by, keeping you out of the battle. You're watching your brothers be slaughtered, and doing nothing to help them. What do you think will happen to you when the Tigris are done with the 11th? Do you think they'll let you leave? Of course not. You'll be wiped out, and that's exactly what Chu wants. If you want to live, join me. You don't have to die here.

"I know that many of you are reluctant to do that, because you've been implanted with a chip. That chip is embedded in your nervous system, and causes blinding pain if you don't do what they tell you," Dryker said, then paused. "We have the means of disabling that chip. Every man that retreats will have that chip removed, and together we'll take down the bastards that did this to you."

Dryker motioned to Celendra, and she tapped her bracelet again. Dryker clasped his hands behind his back, watching the combat. A single orange square broke off from the 11th, then another. A moment later, three squares broke away from the main battlegroup.

Then another handful. Then another. All were headed toward Dryker's fleet.

59

POUNCE

Fizgig smiled grimly as the *Claw* led their fleet into battle. They'd used Tigrana itself to shield their approach, and so far as they knew Mow was oblivious to their presence.

"Izzy, use the planet's gravitational well to accelerate," Fizgig ordered. She dug her claws into one of the cushions, slicing the fabric and exposing the feathers within. The loss of control bothered her, but she wasn't the only one feeling the strain. Khar paced back and forth in front of the weapons station.

Their new crew shifted, all struggling to sit still. This was the pivotal moment, the moment they either stopped Mow, or died in the attempt. Everything hung in the balance, and they all knew it. They'd known it for the past three hours, the length of time it had taken their fleet to circle Tigrana.

They'd prowled the stars the same way their ancestors had prowled the jungles—swift, silent, and deadly. Now they skipped along Tigrana's dense atmosphere, the hull flaring red as they accelerated.

"Mighty Fizgig," Izzy growled over her shoulder. "Our enemy is unaware. Mow's vessel is in the rear, as you predicted. It has a cluster of seven Peregrine-class vessels around it. What are your orders?"

"Fleetwide," Fizgig said, leaping to her feet. She prowled to the screen, her tail lashing back and forth behind her. "Hear me, Pride Fizgig. Pride Leonis has its belly exposed. Bring death to the vessels surrounding the traitor Mow, but leave his death to me. If our enemies surrender, you may accept them as prideless, or slay them if you choose. Teach them to fear our name."

"Mighty Fizgig!" roared Khar, and the cry was taken up by the rest of the bridge crew. Fizgig made no move to silence them, and she shook her head when Izzy looked at her questionably. Let the fleet hear them roar their defiance before battle.

Then they were within visual range. Eight specks gleamed ahead of them, each resolving into a Tigris vessel as they approached. The specks moved slowly, and Fizgig narrowed her eyes when she realized why. They were prowling behind the bulk of the Leonis Pride, watching while their brethren fought and died against the humans killing their home world. She'd known Mow would do it, but seeing it made it more real. And it infuriated her.

Fizgig considered giving Izzy the order to ram, but snapped her mouth shut. That was micromanaging. Izzy was the most skilled pilot she'd ever worked with, and the simplest way to get the result she was after was to let her people do what they were best at.

The *Claw* shuddered as Izzy increased their speed. She tapped a button on her console, and her voice echoed through the corridors of the ship. "Brace for impact. Boarding teams, stand by."

The *Claw* rose, drifting away from Tigrana's atmosphere. They came up low under Mow's ship, at a much greater speed than most would attempt. Fizgig had complete confidence, but most of the rest of the crew had never flown with the snowy-furred prideless. Well, *formerly* prideless.

Crew muttered, and a mangy male who'd lost an ear prayed to Tigrana under his breath. Fizgig smiled, seizing the arms of her chair. She tensed her muscles, watching Mow's vessel grow larger and larger. Its surface gleamed, and Fizgig could already tell what point Izzy had marked. She was aiming for the spot between the two dart ports. It would stab Mow's vessel in the throat. Fitting. If she pulled it off, they would enter the ship near the bridge.

The screen went dark briefly as the entire ship lurched, their momentum suddenly dropping to nothing. The internal dampeners did what they could, but were simply not designed to handle the reduction in velocity.

"To me!" Fizgig roared, her voice thundering across the bridge. She sprinted from the room, up the corridor toward the aft side of the ship.

By the time she reached the boarding tube, two teams had already moved inside. They were a ragtag mix, their armor just as mismatched. The only similarity was the weapon each carried. Each bore one the of the plasma rifles Nolan had given to Fizgig upon her departure.

"Khar?" she asked, purring loudly.

"Yes, Mighty Fizgig," Khar said, stepping forward. "I took the liberty of selecting the best fighters, and outfitting them with Void Wraith technology."

"Well done, Khar," Fizgig said, dropping from the boarding tube to the deck of Mow's ship.

The waiting Tigris scanned the corridor, but there was no obvious threat. Fizgig narrowed her eyes, considering.

Why hadn't Mow opposed them? It made no sense to give up such a potent tactical advantage.

"Mighty Fizgig," Izzy called, her voice coming from above. She dropped soundlessly to the deck next to Fizgig. "The oxygen is lower than it should be. Take a deep breath."

Fizgig did so, and realized immediately what Izzy meant. Her breathing began to quicken. "This isn't impact depressurization. They're pumping the air out of this part of the ship. Move. Move *now*."

She harvested a fresh crop of rage from deep within her belly. Mow was trying to murder them, rather than fight. There could be no more shameless act for a Tigris. This was cowardice, pure and simple.

So Fizgig ran. She knew the layout of Peregrine-class vessels better than any officer living, because she'd served on them for four decades. She pounded across the deck, skidding around a corner and up the next corridor. There was still no opposition, and the longer she ran the more light-headed she became.

Her crew followed, a dozen warriors panting after her. Khar was in the lead, then Izzy. A ten-foot gap opened after them, with her new crew struggling to close it. Fizgig finally slid to a halt when she reached a closed bulkhead. This was where Mow had drawn the line.

"Oxygen," Fizgig gasped, "is on the other side of that door. Get the right side, Khar."

She rested her free paw against the wall next to the door, then flicked her wrist. A crackling blue plasma blade appeared, and Fizgig drove it into the door where it met the deck. Khar realized instantly what she wanted, and started doing the same.

Spots danced across her vision as Fizgig slowly dragged the blade upward. It cut a glowing red arc up the metal, moving inexorably toward the similar arc Khar was carving. Behind her, Fizgig could hear her troops gasping. Most had sagged against the walls, struggling to stay on their feet.

She pulled harder, driving the plasma blade the last six inches. Khar's blade joined their work into an arch, and Fizgig planted her shoulder against the door. She lacked the breath to explain her plan, but fortunately Khar knew what to do. He planted his shoulder next to hers, and they began to push. Nothing. Fizgig tried again, straining against the metal. It was too heavy, and she couldn't think clearly.

Then Izzy was next to her. Then a Tigris she didn't recognize. Then another. Together, they heaved as one. The door slid an inch, two inches. They strained harder, pushing the door into the corridor beyond. There was a sharp pop that made her ears ache, but the pain was welcome. Fizgig drank deep lungfuls as the pressure equalized. They'd done it. Now all they had to do was find Mow.

60

ABJECT LESSON

Chu watched helplessly as another vessel departed, joining the small fleet heading toward Dryker. Less than a third were going, but how long would it be before more decided to join them? No, he needed to stop this. Now.

"Fleetwide," Chu ordered. The new lieutenant, he'd already forgotten her name, nodded when the connection was ready. "All captains, this is Admiral Chu. You are to treat departing vessels as hostile. They are now traitors to the UFC. Eliminate any ship that departs our battlegroup."

Chu settled back into his chair, clutching at his tailbone with both hands. He gritted his teeth against the pain, but it didn't subside. It hadn't. Not for the last several minutes. If anything, it was getting worse.

"Sir, several more vessels have broken off," the tech said.

"On screen," Chu ordered through gritted teeth.

The screen showed four more vessels departing the main battlegroup to join Dryker. The rest of the vessels just let them go, without firing a shot. They were disobeying a direct order. Many of those captains bore a chip, and should have known better.

"I'll just have to remind them of their duty," Chu said, smiling cruelly as he fished the black box from his pocket. It was a master transmitter, linked to hundreds of chips throughout the fleet. Chu considered singling out the captains who were defying him, but decided a more universal lesson was necessary.

He'd remind them all. Chu selected the maximum pain setting, then pressed the tiny red button. He held it in place for a full ten seconds, knowing that every affected soldier was now writhing in agony.

Or they should have been. Chu's officers were chipped, yet beyond a brief flinch not a single one reacted. They stood there, continuing their work as if nothing were happening. Chu stared uncomprehendingly down at the transmitter. Why wasn't it working?

It was impossible for those with implants to suppress the pain. The only reason they'd be on their feet was if the chips weren't getting the signal. For that to happen...

"Someone is jamming the signal," Chu breathed, the realization drowning out the growing pain. He straightened painfully, darting the lieutenant a panicked look. "Withdraw from the fleet. Immediately. Get us to the Helios Gate!"

61

GOTCHA

Nolan watched the battle unfold, aching to intervene. Keeping the harvester cloaked was the single most difficult combat decision he'd ever made. Yet it was the right decision. He needed to be free to act when Chu slipped up, because if they could stop Chu, they freed dozens of captains.

"Captain," Ship said. The sudden voice caused Nolan to jump. He was wound tightly. They all were. "I've just intercepted a signal to the chip. That signal has been neutralized. I've marked the vessel where the signal originated with a white diamond."

Nolan scanned the holomap until he spotted the new icon.

"That's it," Nolan said. "Ship, move to engage. Hannan, as soon as we grapple, this is your show."

Hannan nodded, rising from where she'd been resting against the wall. "We're ready to go whenever. Edwards will guard the boarding tube while the rest of us make the push for the bridge. All three Judicators are standing by."

"Still feels a bit like suicide," Annie said, giving her

plasma blade an experimental wave, then flicking it off. She reached into the pocket of her overalls, shoving a small handful of chew into the corner of her mouth. "At least we've got some damned cool toys."

Nolan ignored them, focusing on the tactical holomap. The ship with the white diamond was breaking away from the mass of orange squares, moving steadily toward the sun. It was at full burn, pushing hard to get away from the battle. Nolan considered that. Why would Chu suddenly break and run? He'd already been in a tactically unwinnable scenario. What had spooked him?

"He knows the chips are disabled," Nolan finally said aloud. "Hannan, I realize this won't change much, but they know we're coming. I'd expect heavy resistance."

"Noted, sir," Hannan said. She withdrew an energy bar and tore the wrapper, then started chewing. "I'm very concerned. This is my concerned face." Her expression was deadpan.

Nolan laughed. Annie joined in. Even Delta smiled. It felt good, though it was short-lived. It trailed off into smiles, and Nolan focused on the holomap once more.

"Ship, how long until intercept?" Nolan asked.

"While under cloak, our maximum speed is reduced. We won't reach the target for three minutes and seventeen seconds," Ship explained. "If we remove our cloak, that will shorten to one minute and forty-two seconds."

"Keep the cloak up," Nolan said, hefting his plasma rifle. "Inform us when we're about to grapple Chu's vessel."

Nolan nodded at Hannan, who turned and walked briskly down the gleaming corridor. They threaded through the ship, working their way down the wing until they were near the tip. Their last three Judicators were already there, each standing at perfect attention. They'd formed a line near the thick blue door leading to the boarding tube.

"I know we all know what to do, but I'm going to run through it one more time, as a sanity check," Nolan said. "Hannan will take point. We'll make our way to the bridge, trying to avoid any resistance while we do. No shots fired, unless we have no other choice. Once we reach the bridge, we'll locate Chu and neutralize him. Ideally we take him alive, but if we can't that's fine."

"You left out the part about escaping," Annie said, spitting a gob of black into the corner. "How are we getting out, with or without Chu?"

"That part you aren't going to much like," Nolan said, glancing at Delta. The big black man lurked near the Judicators, watching. "When we take Chu, we need to take his transmitter. Chu is a paranoid bastard, and I'm betting most or even all of his crew are chipped."

"So you're going to do the same thing Chu did to break them?" Delta asked. His tone was neutral, but Nolan didn't think it was accidental that Delta's hand dropped to his plasma pistol.

"Only if we have to. There's every chance his crew will defect once they see Chu go down, but if they don't I'll use the chips, yes," Nolan said. His mouth firmed to a tight line. "I need to know you can handle that, Delta. If it's our lives, I'll do what I have to do. There's more than just us riding on the line here. Either we win, or they do. If they win, a whole lot more people are going to be chipped. Or worse. If I need to get my hands a little dirty to stop that, I'm doing it."

"Fine," Delta snarled, turning to face the blue metal door. Nolan felt Hannan relax behind him. She'd coiled like a spring, no doubt ready to take Delta down if he'd proven to be a threat. Nolan was glad it hadn't come to that.

"Captain, impact in seven seconds," Ship said, cheerfully.

Nolan braced himself against the wall, and the others did the same. There was a shudder as they impacted, but it wasn't nearly as bad as he'd been expecting. The Judicators didn't brace themselves at all, rolling with the vibration like sailors at sea.

The door slid up, revealing the inside of Chu's flagship. The clean corridors reminded Nolan of a higher-tech version of the *UFC Johnston*, which stoked his anger. Her death could be laid at Chu's feet.

"All right, Hannan," Nolan said, turning to face the shorter Marine. "This is your show."

62

WRATH OF THE PRIDELESS

Fizgig panted as she faced the war horde behind her. A dozen Tigris warriors in mismatched armor, each holding one of the most devastating weapons in the galaxy. Mow had the advantage of training, but she had firepower.

"Ready yourselves for battle," Fizgig growled, loudly enough to be heard by those close to her, but not a full shout. No need to advertise themselves to Mow's warriors. Not just yet, anyway. "Beyond this point, we will be assaulted by the best Leonis has to offer. These Tigris are battle-hardened, and they will die before surrendering. Cut them down. Show no mercy."

Then Fizgig gave the door one final heave. It toppled inward, clattering to the deck with a boom that echoed through the ship. Beyond it, as expected, crouched several Tigris warriors. They wore black armor, and each carried a polished black shotgun.

Even as they began raising their weapons, Fizgig was firing. She let off two bursts of plasma, each catching one of the waiting Tigris in the chest. They toppled to the deck screaming, their armor turning molten from the shots. They struggled to remove it, but the armor had melted too much to allow them to release it. It was a horrible way to die.

Before Fizgig could fire again, Khar was pushing up the corridor, firing repeatedly. Two more enemy Tigris dropped, but several others took aim and fired. Khar staggered back, his armor catching the worst of the shots. One caught him on his unprotected forearm, and he gave a roar of pained rage. He charged forward, igniting his plasma blade as he came down on the Tigris who'd shot him.

The shorter female brought up her rifle to block, but Khar's weapon sliced through the metal. His humming blade continued, slicing through the flesh where her neck and shoulder met. She collapsed to the deck in a spray of blood that drenched Khar.

Two more Tigris shot Khar, and he fell to the deck. Fizgig began moving to intercept, but Izzy was already there. The snowy white Tigris darted forward, a plasma pistol in each hand. She let off a flurry of shots, dropping the two Tigris seeking to pounce on Khar.

The battle dissolved into chaos, as Tigris on both sides closed to melee. Screams and roars sounded all around Fizgig as she glided into combat. She gave in to her feral instincts, cutting down foes as quickly as they appeared. She had no idea how much time had passed by the time the battle haze faded.

Fizgig looked around, panting heavily. Several of her new crew were down, but most were still up. Over a dozen enemy bodies littered the deck around them. Now it was time to advertise their presence, to let their enemies know that death approached.

"Look!" Fizgig roared, pointing at the corpses littering the corridor. "They are the best Leonis have to offer. They carry the honor of the pride. Yet you, prideless a day ago, have slaughtered them on their own vessel. We. Are. *Mighty.*"

The warriors around her took up the cry, howling their fury until it echoed down the corridor, and through the rest of the ship. Fizgig let it go on for long seconds, long enough that every last Leonis would hear. Then she raised a fist. Silence took longer than it should have, but it came after a few moments.

"We make for the bridge," Fizgig said, turning to face her people. "It is time to end this."

63

I DON'T THINK SO

"Listen up," Hannan snapped, in her best drill sergeant voice. Annie, Delta, the captain, and even the Judicators snapped to attention. "Keep five feet between you and the next person. Move quickly and quietly. No speaking unless we're about to be attacked. Any questions?"

"Nah, but since I can't go make sure you bring me a souvenir," Edwards said, waving with his remaining arm. He'd taken up a defensive position, and Hannan felt a little bad for anyone that stepped into his firing arc.

Everyone else shook their heads, so Hannan strode into the docking tube. She pressed the button on the top of her belt buckle, wincing as the itchy feeling settled over her skin. Moving at a fast walk, she hurried up the corridor and away from the entry point.

Since their vessel had been cloaked when they'd attacked, the enemy soldiers would have been caught off guard. They'd have no way of knowing where the breach point was, and it would take a squad of Marines at least two more minutes to locate it. By then, she wanted to be far away from here.

Hannan hugged the aft corridor, circling along the outside of the ship. It wasn't the fastest way to the bridge, but it was also a whole lot less predictable. Hopefully, Chu's Marines wouldn't even know they'd been boarded until Hannan's squad burst onto the bridge.

They made their way slowly, eventually reaching a lift. Hannan paused beside it, looking down one side of the corridor, then the other. She moved over to the shimmer she was sure belonged to the captain, then breathed softly in his direction. "If we take the lift to level A, they may see it coming."

"Do it," the captain whispered back. "Speed matters as much as stealth."

Hannan tapped the button next to the lift, filing inside when the doors opened. Other shimmering figures pressed in behind her, and she frowned as the doors slid shut. The cloaks were potent, but in an enclosed area like this they wouldn't matter. This was basically a kill box, and when the doors opened it was quite possible Chu would have soldiers waiting.

"Switch your stealth field to shield," Hannan ordered, turning a dial atop her belt buckle. She shimmered back into view, and the others did the same. "Captain, Annie, take a knee. Delta and I will fire over you."

Everyone took their positions, two ranks ready to fire the instant the door opened. They waited tensely, and Hannan realized she was holding her breath. She forced herself to breathe normally, resting her index finger on the plasma rifle's trigger guard as she waited for the doors to open.

Ding.

The doors slid open, and a thunder of automatic weapons fire began. Bullets filled the tiny elevator, and Hannan was knocked back a step from impacts. She recovered quickly, firing wild bursts of plasma into the mass of UFC soldiers standing about twenty feet back from the elevator. Fortunately, they hadn't had time to erect any sort of cover. Hannan wasn't sure it would have mattered, given how lethal the plasma fire could be.

Her first shot caught a man in the leg, spilling him to the deck with a screech of agony. She fired again, conscious of the others doing the same. Their shields protected them from the slug-throwing weapons, providing an unfair advantage. They were gunning down opponents quickly, and Hannan couldn't help but feel like it was a little too easy.

"Grenade!" the captain roared, rolling out of the elevator. Annie scrambled out as well, and Delta vaulted over them.

Hannan was right behind them, but moved a second too slowly. The black, fist-sized grenade detonated, hurling her into the air. The concussive force carried her into the waiting soldiers, and her wild flight knocked two of them prone. Thankfully, her shield protected her from the worst of the blast. The landing knocked the wind from her, but she was still mobile.

Hannan flipped to her stomach, then pulled herself into a crouch. Most of the remaining soldiers were trying to deal with the captain, who gunned them down as quickly as he could take aim. A few turned toward her, just in time for her to raise her plasma rifle and start firing. *Tap, tap, tap.* Three more soldiers dropped.

Just like that, all opponents were down. "Well done, all."

"There goes the element of surprise," Nolan said, helping Annie to her feet. "Getting to the bridge is going to be tough."

"At least we don't have far to go," Hannan said, gesturing at the corridor running along the stern. "They've probably got one more line of defense waiting, and after that we'll be onto the bridge itself. We'll have to move quickly, though. I'm sure word is going out to every fire team on the ship to converge on the bridge."

"Then let's get moving," Nolan said, starting up the corridor.

64

DRYKER

"Move us closer to the 11th," Dryker ordered, pacing back and forth as he studied the battle. "Order all the ships joining us to cluster behind the Primo, and have your vessels form a line. Move them slowly toward the battle."

"As you wish, Admiral," Celendra said, but there was a note of dissent in her voice.

"You have a comment on my orders?" Dryker asked, probably more defensively than he should have.

"The Primo are not here to get involved in your war, Admiral. Asking us to approach the battle is dangerous," Celendra said, mouth turning down into a tiny scowl.

"Put me on an open channel to all races," Dryker ordered. He didn't bother addressing her comment, because she was right. He *was* risking the Primo. It was the last card he had to play.

"Done," Celendra said, looking away from him. She stalked to the far side of the dais, barely within earshot. It was the angriest he'd seen her.

"Attention, vessels of the 11th fleet, and vessels of the

Leonis Pride. Disengage, or you will both be fired upon," Dryker ordered. He paused, then added a bit more weight. "You all know what Primo weaponry can do. The vessels of the 14th have been outfitted with plasma cannons. Cease. Fire."

Now all Dryker could do was wait. He stared at the sea of triangles and squares crawling across the screen. The Tigris and the humans were in the thick of it, tearing each other apart. It would be difficult to disengage, and even if captains were willing, they might not have a choice but to continue fighting.

He straightened, staring hard as he saw new movement. Seven ships in the 11th's backline were breaking off and heading in his direction. That was nearly a quarter of the remaining human vessels.

"Dryker, is that you?" a friendly voice called. It called to mind late-night poker games in the *Johnston*'s officer lounge.

"Hello, Captain Lang," Dryker said, smiling in spite of himself. Sarah had been the only officer he'd ever seen escape the 14th. She'd been the reason there was an opening for Nolan. "I'm glad you and your companions are willing to see reason."

"Command has had some pretty odd orders lately, and this isn't what we signed on for. Might be we're committing mutiny, but I can't be a party to this, and most of the 11th feels the same way," she explained over the comm. "I don't know that they'll be able to break away though. They're getting pounded, and if you can't get the cats to play nice, they're going to slaughter most of my people."

Dryker clenched a fist, looking at the beleaguered 11th. Their lines were collapsing, and the Tigris showed no sign of breaking off.

65

MOW

F izgig kicked off the bulkhead, twisting in midair to deliver a quick strike with her plasma blade. It severed the unsuspecting male's spinal cord, punching through armor and bone alike. He slumped to the deck as she landed on the other side of his body.

"Mowwwwww," she howled up the corridor. They were closing on the bridge, and she knew he was close enough to hear her. "I'm coming for you. Tell your warriors to stand aside, or I will cut down every last one."

The only answer was a shotgun blast from a single Tigris warrior sheltering behind the corner. Fizgig dropped prone, and the blast cratered the wall behind her. Before she could rise, Khar leapt forward, sprinting down the hall.

The warrior with the shotgun popped out of cover for another shot, just in time for Khar to plant his plasma blade in the warrior's skull. The white-furred beast gave a brief cry, the smell of burnt fur filling the corridor as he died.

"Mighty Fizgig," Khar called, peering around the corner. "The bridge is directly ahead. They are well fortified."

Fizgig walked calmly to Khar's side, aware of the cluster

of warriors behind her. Only five were still with her. Five, out of the dozen who'd started out. Yet they'd killed three times their number, a full thirty-six of Leonis' best warriors. It was a legendary assault, one for the annals.

"Leonis Pride warriors!" Fizgig roared, her voice echoing down the hall. "Mow is a coward. First, he cut off life support. When we escaped, he sent dozens of your brothers and sisters to die, all to avoid my challenge. All are dead now, at *my* hand. Are you Tigris? Do you not follow the strongest warrior? If Mow is your leader, then let him face me. Put down your arms, and we will accept your surrender. Let Mow fight, instead of cowering behind proud Leonis warriors."

Khar gave her an approving nod, his tail rising, even as his chest puffed out. "Well said, Mighty Fizgig."

"Mow has been challenged," boomed a voice from the bridge. "We know Mighty Fizgig. Some of us have fought beside her. She is honorable, and it is not right that Mow has refused this challenge. If he is truly the warrior he claims to be, truly worthy of leading Leonis, then let him step forward and fight."

She recognized that voice. It was Kallas. She'd served under Fizgig's first command, three decades prior. Fizgig smiled, waiting for the inevitable. After several moments, a rhythmic stomping began from the bridge. Fizgig took it up, as did the the warriors around her. It spread from warrior to warrior, until the thud of a hundred feet echoed around them.

Fizgig stepped from cover, walking proudly onto the bridge. There was a chance that this was a trick, but she refused to believe it. No one would dishonor a formal challenge, except perhaps for Mow. She took a deep breath as she passed onto the bridge's command deck.

A dozen warriors dotted the room, every last one of them stomping. The only one not stomping was the male in the captain's chair. Mow's eyes blazed as he stared at her. His mane had more white in it than the last she'd seen him. He rose slowly to his feet, taking a step down to the command deck. The stomping stopped, plunging the bridge into relative silence.

"You've endangered our race for the last time. Even now our world burns, yet you seek challenge? Very well," Mow said, stalking toward her. "I accept your challenge. I will eat your heart, Fizgig."

66

THE BRIDGE

N olan panted as he rested against the wall next to the wide hatch leading to the next room. He was less winded than he'd have been a few months ago, but the constant combat was still taking a toll. It just underscored how much more conditioning he really needed.

"These should be handy," Hannan said, picking up a pair of grenades from one of the corpses.

She walked to the hatch where Nolan crouched, popped the pin, then threw the grenade. It pinged off the wall, clinked its way into the distance. There was a sudden scramble of footsteps pounding across the deck from that direction.

"Grenade," someone yelled.

"Take cover," someone else yelled at the same time.

By the time the grenade detonated, Hannan was sprinting around the corner. She slowed her advance when they reached the next corner, peeking around with her rifle. She fired a quick shot, then ducked back behind cover.

"There are at least eight of them, probably closer to a

dozen," Hannan said. "They've erected full barricades, and
are using them as cover. Chu was expecting an attack."

"Doesn't change anything, unfortunately," Nolan said,
dropping to one knee and taking a quick peek around the
corner. He ducked back, and an instant later a rifle cracked.
The bullet glanced off the wall right next to where his face
had been. Nolan glanced up at Hannan. "How do you want
to approach this?"

"Well, we've still got our friends," she said, nodding at
the trio of Judicators. Thus far, the Judicators had mostly
hung back, picking off targets of opportunity.

"Sounds like as good a use as any," Nolan said, turning to
the Judicators. "You three, move around that corner, and cut
down all defenders."

Hannan popped the second pin, lobbing it around the
corner. Nolan held up a hand, and the Judicators waited.
When the grenade detonated, Hannan motioned for the
Judicators to move forward, and move they did. They faded
from sight, their cloaked forms firing the instant they'd
rounded the corner.

"Give it a three count," Hannan said. "Then we're going
to rush in and pick up the pieces."

The telltale plasma fire of Judicators came from around
the corner, followed by automatic weapons fire. Nolan was
relieved to be on this side of the Judicators, as he remembered how terrifying they'd been when they boarded the
Johnston. He only wished he had more than three to
work with.

Hannan leaped from cover, darting around the corner.
The instant she disappeared from sight, he caught the
bright flash of plasma as she engaged the enemy. Delta and
Annie were next, each adding their weapons into the mix.

Then it was Nolan's turn, and he leapt into the fray. He

scanned the situation, the moment seeming to stretch as his mind catalogued targets. Seven Marines dotted the three barricades on the other side of the door leading onto the bridge. The barricades were waist-high, and each Marine was taking advantage of that cover. Hannan had moved to one side of the hallway, Delta and Annie the other. All three were lobbing potshots at the barricade, areas of white ferro-concrete flowing like lava where their blasts hit.

The defending Marines kept up a steady staccato of fire. The lead Judicator had taken the brunt of that fire, but made it as far as the first barricade before going down. It leapt forward, its body straddling the barricade. Nolan expected the Marines to scatter, but they seemed unaware of the danger in their midst. They'd never fought Void Wraith.

He raised his rifle, firing a trio of hasty shots as he dropped into cover behind Hannan. The remaining two Judicators went down under withering fire, leaving Nolan and Hannan untouched. More importantly, it left them in the comparative shelter of the hallway.

The first Judicator detonated, sending Marines, parts of the barricade, and metallic debris in all directions. A moment later the second and third Judicators went up, finishing the grisly work. Nolan stood up slowly, realizing none of the Marines were moving.

They'd reached the bridge. It was time to deal with Chu.

67

THE CHALLENGE

Fizgig studied Mow, watching the old cat circle warily. Mow moved like a younger cat, but there was an underlying tremor there. His golden fur had faded to a soft dun, and he didn't look so much old as he did...unhealthy. There was something wrong with him, something lurking just beyond the edge of his scent.

"Mighty Mow," a golden-furred male boomed. "You have been challenged. How will you fight?"

"Claw-to-claw," Mow said, eyes narrowing as he met Fizgig's gaze. "I want to feel your life fading. I will serve your blood to my kits in their milk, Fizgig. When I am done your name will be scoured from the sacred scrolls."

Fizgig nodded stoically. She tossed her plasma rifle to Khar, then unbuckled the bracelet from her wrist. She'd have preferred to use the plasma blade, but Mow had the right to set the terms. He'd quite wisely chosen equal footing, as he'd have had no chance against Void Wraith tech.

Claw-to-claw was another matter. Mow was larger than Fizgig, though she was undoubtedly faster. He'd taught her much of what she knew about fighting, and their styles were still quite similar. This would be the most challenging fight of her career, with the most riding on it. So Fizgig cleared her mind, and focused on the battle.

Mow closed until he stood a bare three feet away. His breath was fetid, his gaze fevered. Fizgig's revulsion was palatable, and she resisted the urge to retreat a step. That would be taken as a sign of weakness, and she couldn't afford that.

"A challenge has been issued and accepted," the golden-furred male boomed. He raised both paws, one over Fizgig, and the other Mow. "When my paws descend, battle will be joined. Fight well and with cunning." The warrior stepped back, lowering his paws with a flourish.

Fizgig lunged, launching a swipe at Mow's throat. Speed was her only ally, after all.

Mow shocked her, moving with explosive speed. He seized her wrist with an expression of disdain. He held her for a moment, then twisted her arm with a painful crack. Fizgig howled in agony as the bone broke the skin. Mow still held her, twisting just enough to prevent her attempts to free herself. He was far stronger than any Tigris had a right to be.

"You are weak, Fizgig," Mow said. "You always we—"

Fizgig went berserk. All the pain, all the frustration. All the humiliation, and the sadness. She channeled it all, whipping both legs up and wrapping them around Mow's neck. He tried to step back, but since he was holding her aloft he merely carried her with him.

Fizgig tightened her legs, putting immense pressure on Mow's windpipe. He released her arm, digging his claws into her leg. They dug deep, carving into the muscle as he slashed at her. She ignored the pain, swiping upward with her good hand. It caught Mow in the face, and her pinky claw pierced his right eye with a terrible pop. Mow screeched, tumbling to the deck with Fizgig atop him.

She tried to scramble backwards, knowing her injuries were crippling. Mow wouldn't let her. He seized the scruff of her neck with a paw, yanking her back. Mow leapt atop her, using his superior weight and strength. She struggled, but her right leg refused to obey her. The muscles in her thigh must have been shredded by Mow's attack. Her right arm was a shattered mass. She squirmed, but Mow held her, seemingly without effort. All she was able to manage was twisting to look him in the eye.

That eye made her blink. Green, viscous fluid leaked from the socket. Nor was she the only one who saw it. Mutters went up around the room, mutters about Mow being some sort of monster. Mow glanced around the room with his good eye, as if daring someone to say something.

In that instant Fizgig saw her chance. She lunged upwards, using her good arm to push herself up. Her fangs closed around Mow's throat, and she bit down with all her strength. Hot, disgusting fluid filled her mouth. It wasn't blood—or it wasn't only blood. Whatever was mixed in was the foulest thing Fizgig had ever tasted, and she longed to spit it out. Instead, she bit down harder.

Mow's paws shot to her shoulder, and he pushed down with all his might. He was so strong, monstrously so. Unfortunately for him, Fizgig had him in a death grip. When he forced her head down, it ripped Fizgig away from his neck, tearing out his throat in the process. Mow stumbled back from her, clutching his ruined neck with both hands.

He looked around the deck for support, finding none. Every Tigris averted their gaze, until Mow sagged to his knees. Fizgig used that to give her strength. She pulled herself to her feet, standing on her uninjured leg. Only leaning against the bulkhead prevented her from falling.

"I do not know what you've become, Mow, but you are no longer Tigris," Fizgig said, spitting a mouthful of blood onto the deck. She turned to the golden-furred warrior who'd adjudicated the fight. "You are his first?"

"Yes, Mighty Fizgig," the male said, nodding deferentially.

"Broadcast the fight to the Tigris fleet," she ordered, limping to the captain's chair. She sat heavily, not even looking when Mow's body toppled to the deck. A pool of green spread out from his body, proof of whatever physical change the Void Wraith had wrought.

"Connection established, Mighty Fizgig. They are receiving the vid of the fight now," the male said. She should learn his name, but she was too weary, and in too much pain. It would be weeks, perhaps months, before she recovered from this fight. If she ever did.

"Give me an open channel as soon as the footage has played," Fizgig ordered, aware that her words were beginning to slur. She battled past the pain, trying to remain conscious.

"Done," the male said.

"Tigris of the Leonis Pride," she said. "As you can see, I have bested Mow. As you can also see from his unclean blood, Mow has been corrupted by the Void Wraith. It is they who have forced us to war, they who have burned Tigrana." She paused for a moment as the pain became too great to continue. Sheer will drew forth the next few words. "Cease combat. Fall back to join my fleet, or be branded traitors and hunted down."

68

UM, EWW

T he Bridge of Chu's flagship was nearly deserted, at least compared to an older ship like the *UFC Johnston*. A handful of officers cowered behind blocky stations, clearly trying to avoid Nolan's attention. He doubted they'd be a problem, but it was better not to take chances.

"Hannan, get someone on those techs," Nolan ordered, prowling across the deck toward a raised platform that butted against the rear wall.

A single chair sat atop that platform, aimed at the largest view screen Nolan had ever seen on a human vessel. Currently, that screen showed the battle raging in the system behind them. Curls of white-hot flame drifted past, evidence of how close they were to the star's corona.

"This place creeps me the hell out. These people look like war refugees. They'd wet themselves if we said boo," Hannan said, stepping up to join Nolan. Her rifle was still at her shoulder, barrel still trained on the techs.

Annie had settled into a crouch behind one of the largest remaining pieces of the barricade. Delta picked a path through the wreckage, his rifle cradled absently in his left hand. He stopped a few feet behind Nolan, his emotionless eyes scanning the room.

"Ahh," a wheezy voice called, as the chair on the platform swiveled to face them. "You must be Commander Nolan. Mendez has told me quite a lot about you. Did you know that he was your greatest supporter? He wanted to give you a ship. Mendez knew something was up, that someone was infiltrating the admiralty. He was convinced you'd be able to sniff out the traitors."

Chu's skin was translucent, a stark contrast to the dark red veins covering most of his skin. Nolan had no idea what they were, but he was positive it had something to do with the larva. The same larva that was growing inside Kathryn.

"Your guards are dead," Nolan said, raising his rifle as he approached. "Give us the chip transmitter, and surrender yourself into our custody. We have Void Wraith facilities. We can treat this. You don't have to die."

"Don't have to die?" Chu said, laughing uproariously. It sputtered off into coughing, and a thick stream of green and black blood ran from the corner of Chu's mouth. "I'm already dead, you fool. Sacrificed on the altar of the masters. I give birth to the future."

His body began to writhe, then to tremble violently.

"Fall back to the barricade!" Nolan roared, backpedaling. He kept his eyes on Chu's body, his rifle aimed at the man's face.

Delta raised his rifle and fired a blob of blue-white plasma that disintegrated Chu's head. Nolan was about to chastise him, but held his tongue when the body continued to writhe. If anything, that writhing became more violent. Nolan risked a glance back. Hannan and Annie had taken cover, but Delta hadn't moved.

Nolan was about to grab him by the shoulder when a tendril of ropy ligament shot from Chu's body, a mass of thinner tendrils at one end grasping like fingers. The tendril shot directly for Delta's face. Nolan lowered the rifle with his left hand, even as his right hand shot up. He flicked his wrist to ignite the plasma blade, slashing at the tendril just before it grabbed Delta. The blade sent of a spray of greenish blood as it lopped the end off the tendril.

Delta backpedaled, firing wildly at the admiral's corpse. More tendrils shot out, and Nolan narrowly avoided one aimed at his leg. He turned and sprinted, careful to keep out of Hannan's firing arc as she and Annie opened fire.

"That thing is growing fast," Hannan said, as Nolan dove into cover next to her. "What the hell do we do?"

Nolan looked up to see the ropy tendrils covering the entire platform. Thick membranes flowed between them, growing into leathery walls. It was all happening with alarming speed.

"My God," Nolan muttered. "I think that thing is a cocoon."

69

CHRYSALIS

Nolan added his fire to the rest of the squad's, disintegrating tendrils as the cocoon tried to spread. The tendrils were getting longer, and he watched in horror as they shot into the navigation area. The hapless crew techs were unprepared, struggling to flee as the tendrils wrapped around their legs. They were dragged back toward the cocoon with supernatural speed.

"Don't let it get those techs," Nolan barked, pivoting and firing his rifle. He severed the closest cable, and the tech tumbled to the deck. Three more tendrils shot out, latching around the man.

The rest of the squad pivoted as well, adding their fire to his. There were just too many tendrils. For every one they severed, two more emerged. Nolan knew the strategy wasn't working. That cocoon was feeding, and he didn't want to see what it would do with that much biomass. His gut tightened, but he gave the order anyway.

"Kill the technicians," Nolan yelled, shifting to fire at the man he'd been trying to save. Two shots vaporized most of his body, but the tendrils greedily snapped up the remains, dragging them back into the main mass.

The rest of the squad dealt with the remaining bridge crew, each paying their own emotional price. Then they shifted their fire back to the main body. Its growth had slowed, but it had managed to erect some kind of thick, fleshy membrane. Their shots pierced it, but the membrane grew back as quickly as it was destroyed.

"Sir, how the hell do we kill this thing?" Hannan yelled, still firing.

"Not sure yet," Nolan yelled back. "Keep firing while I figure it out."

Nolan mind began deciphering the problem. This was analysis, the thing he most excelled at. How did this life form work? How did they kill it? Presumably the thing had a brain of some kind, a vulnerable structure that commanded the body. But where would that be located? He considered Kathryn's scans. The larva gestated around the tailbone, working its way up the spine, until it dominated the entire central nervous system.

He wasn't positive, but it seemed likely that if any part of this thing was the brain, it would be the place where the larva gestated.

"Okay," Nolan yelled to the squad. He rose from cover, advancing on the cocoon. "Form up on me."

"You want us to get closer to that thing?" Hannan yelled. "You're nuts, sir."

"I'm with Hannan," Annie said. "There any reason we can't just flee and blow us the ship?"

"Yeah," Nolan said. "We need the transmitter, so we can free every officer in the fleet. Leaving without that isn't an option. We're going to attack the body in a coordinated assault. Annie and Hannan, keep the tendrils at bay. Delta, carve a path inside the thing. We need to reach Chu's body. When we do, I'm going to try to kill it."

Delta nodded, moving to point and slowly advancing on the creature. Their withering barrage of fire kept the tendrils at bay, though Nolan had to dodge more than one that got a little too close. They pressed forward, inching their way closer as Delta used his rifle to create a hole in the membrane. He kept firing, widening the hole even as the creature struggled to close it. Nolan added his fire to Delta's, ensuring that they outpaced the regeneration.

Then they finally passed inside the thing, ducking through the membrane, and into a jungle of tendrils. They snaked from floor to ceiling and wall to wall, a fleshy lattice-work. Nolan ignited his plasma blade, and joined Delta in cutting a path.

"Over there," Delta said, pointing through the mass of tendrils. "Chu's body."

"Hannan, Annie, stay back and use your rifles. Destroy anything moving in our direction," Nolan said, creeping after Delta. They slashed their way across the last few feet, and had almost reached the corpse when a dozen tendrils all leapt at Delta. Plasma fire caught a few of them, but the rest wrapped around the big man, pulling him tight. One wrapped around his throat, cutting off the panicked scream.

Time slowed as Nolan's gaze alternated between Delta and Chu. The admiral's body was just a few feet away.

"Do it," Delta choked out.

Nolan nodded, darting toward Chu. He jerked his arm back, then plunged the plasma blade into Chu's lower spine. He did it over and over, quick motions that tore and cooked the surrounding tissue.

A high pitched squeal on the edge of hearing knocked Nolan to his knees, but he shook it off and kept stabbing.

The keening wail grew weaker, then finally ceased. Nolan kept stabbing. The tendrils all around him went limp. Nolan turned off his blade and pulled out his sidearm. He held it ready to fire as he explored Chu's pockets. It was grisly, but Nolan forced himself to keep searching until he found a small black box.

The tendrils were still silent. Nolan leaned back, vaporizing Chu with three precise shots, then turned to see Hannan helping Delta free of the tendrils.

"Let's get the hell out of here," Nolan said.

70

AFTERMATH

D ryker's hands were clenched into fists as he watched the battle unfolding. Casualties had been enormously high on both sides, and only a few dozen ships outside his fleet were still fighting. Most of the 11th had been destroyed, and the Leonis had paid a high price for it.

"Admiral," Celendra said, blinking. "Fizgig has just defeated the Leonis commander. As I understand it, she is now in command."

Dryker watched as the remaining Tigris vessels disengaged from the 11th. They limped their way back to the tiny Tigris fleet Fizgig had arrived with. Even after every vessel had made it back to Fizgig, there were still only three dozen. Thirty-six, out of over a hundred that had arrived.

The few 11th fleet vessels that were able to limped to Dryker's side, joining his own tiny fleet. He did a quick scan, counting seventy-one vessels. That meant that outside of the 14th, only about thirty ships had survived.

"Shall we intervene with Chu's vessel?" Celendra asked,

gesturing at a pair of blue diamonds at the very edge of the sun's corona.

"I'm sure Nolan has it well in hand, but we'll take the *First Light* to assist. Give me fleetwide, open frequency," Dryker ordered.

Celendra nodded a moment later, wiping at a bead of green liquid leaking from her eye. The Primo version of a cold, maybe? Celendra had seemed increasingly unwell over the last few days.

"This is Admiral Dryker, and I'm addressing everyone who can hear this. Humans. Tigris. Primo. Everyone has a stake in what happened here today," Dryker said. "The Void Wraith won a great victory. They've severely damaged our military—all three militaries. But we've won a victory too. They didn't wipe us out, and those who survive are ready to fight back. To fight back as a united group.

"I invite the Tigris commander and all fleet captains to join us aboard the *First Light*," Dryker continued. "We'll schedule the meeting for tomorrow at noon. In the meantime, tend to your wounded, and bury your dead. Today we mourn. Tomorrow we go to war."

Dryker nodded at Celendra and she severed the connection.

71

UNEXPECTED COMPLICATIONS

The Eye observed many things, floating in the darkness near the life-giving star that was ever-so-slowly being pulled into the supermassive black hole at the center of the Milky Way. A thousand thousand vessels dotted this galaxy, each linked to the Eye through one of the larvae that would one day become true Gorthians.

Two vessels in particular had captivated the Eye's attention, both witnessing unexpected events. Such events were rare, though they'd been increasingly common since entity Nolan had become involved.

The Eye watched as its progeny was nearly born from the body of vessel Chu, then slain by entity Nolan. It watched as vessel Celendra spoke to Dryker, discussing the battle that had devastated their fleets. More of those fleets survived than should have, and the fact that entity Dryker was unifying all three races into a single cohesive fighting force was troubling.

Troubling...and intriguing. The Eye had learned much, watching entity Dryker through vessel Celendra's eyes.

Entity Dryker was bold, cunning, and decisive. He demonstrated everything that made his species ideal servants.

The Tigris were powerful, aggressive warriors. They
made excellent troops, perhaps even more so than the
Primo. They had the added benefit of comparatively rapid
reproduction, making them more ideal slaves than the
Primo. Yet humanity eclipsed them both. They bred quickly,
were highly aggressive, yet also demonstrated the ability to
consider problems differently.

They were unpredictable, intelligent, and tenacious.
They'd made perfect slaves, particularly as officers and
commanders. Initial reports indicated there were over
seventy billion of them, a sizable contingent if they could all
be harvested. Add in the Tigris, and this harvest might be
the best in history. The masters would be pleased.

Thankfully, entity Dryker seemed unaware that vessel
Celendra had been infected. The Eye had ordered her larva
to take no action that might call attention to itself, as the
intelligence she passed was far more valuable than the short
term havoc she could wreak. That might change, in time,
but until it did he would continue to monitor entity Dryker's
progress.

An unquiet voice reminded the Eye of the only harvest
that might rival this one, the harvest in which it had first
encountered the Primo. Those Primo had possessed technology most races never amassed, and had used that technology to devastating effect. The speed with which they'd
created and modified new weapons was unparalleled, and
the Eye was painfully aware that their greatest achievement
was still out there somewhere, in some forgotten corner of
space. Waiting for discovery.

That was what had brought it to this system, after all.
Somewhere near the supermassive black hole lay the Birth-

place, the research station where the Primo had created the Forge, the only vessel that had defeated every Void Wraith fleet sent to destroy it.

Still, that was a minor variable. Nearly fifty millennia had passed, and no one had discovered the ship. Even if they did, the Eye had countless contingency plans. It focused its attention on the vessels commanding its fleets. It saw them all simultaneously, over four thousand Void Wraith harvesters. Those fleets were superior to both humanity and the Tigris. They were the equal of the Primo, and they outnumbered them nearly a hundred to one.

Victory was all but assured. The chance of any other outcome was a statistical impossibility. The masters would be pleased.

72

MEETINGS

Dryker was more than a little nervous, walking the corridors of the Void Wraith vessel. It had belonged to the enemy, and the fact that Nolan was in charge now didn't banish the sense of unease at being here. Yet it made sense. If they used the *First Light*, or even the *Claw of Tigrana*, then there would be warriors, technicians, and other crew there. Those people, any of whom could be a spy, would witness the outcome of this historic meeting, and right now secrecy was paramount.

Dryker was the last to enter. Celendra was seated at the far end of the room, awkwardly straddling a chair designed for humans. Fizgig sat two chairs down, her ears flicking as she groomed the fur around the cast on her arm. She wore a similar cast on her leg, both made from quick-sealing foam. It was very similar to what humans used to set bones.

Nolan was there, too, of course. He sat at the head of the table, giving Dryker a respectful nod. It was a gesture one gave an equal, not a superior. Dryker smiled, returning the nod, then walked to the other end of the table to take a seat.

"I'm sorry I'm late," he said, undoing the top button on

his uniform. "There are more Fleet logistics than I'd have expected. If not for Lieutenant Juliard, I'd still be there."

"We are beyond pleasantries," Fizgig said, flexing her claws and digging them into the metal table. "Let us discuss what has brought us here. We three represent the significant factions: Dryker the humans, Celendra the Primo, and myself the Tigris."

"You're the leader of Leonis Pride?" Nolan asked. He didn't seem surprised, more like he was correlating a bit of data he'd already known.

To Dryker's immense surprise, Fizgig shook her head and looked down at the table. "No," she said a moment later, and looked up. "I turned down that honor. In order to stop Mow, I was forced to do something that has not been done in nearly two centuries: I've founded my own pride. Every prideless was invited, and now that we are pride I cannot abandon them."

"But you still speak for the Tigris?" Dryker asked.

"For two prides, at least," Fizgig said, her tail rising. "Leonis has not chosen a leader, but I speak for them until they do."

"What of the rest of the prides?" Celendra asked, blinking. "Are there not close to a dozen more?"

"Most of those are small, and those that are not are unlikely to seek alliance," Fizgig said, her irises narrowing to slits. "I will do what I can to bring them into the fold, but I make no promises."

"Some Tigris are better than none. Well done, Fizgig," Dryker said, resting his elbows on the table. "Now that we've dealt with pleasantries, let's get to business, as Fizgig suggests. We're not here to discuss troop dispositions, or combat strength. We're screwed, and we know it. Our combined fleets aren't strong enough to police known space, meaning the Void Wraith get to pick the playing field. We can only react, and we all know how that will end. They'll pick off our colonies one by one, until we have only the core worlds. Then they'll take those, too."

Dryker stopped there, though he could have added quite a bit more about current circumstances. He was especially interested in Nolan's report, and in his opinion on stopping the Void Wraith. Dryker had no idea how they were going to do that, but the kid was a tactical genius.

"If we are not here to discuss military deployment, then why are we here, Admiral Dryker?" Celendra asked. She wiped milky sweat from her forehead, blinking in what Dryker took for exhaustion.

"To stop the Void Wraith," Nolan supplied, drawing her attention. "As you saw from my report, I've learned quite a bit about them, and about their physiology. More importantly, we've learned about their history. The ancient Primo resisted them, and they did so using a vessel they called the Forge. It's the source of their technical miracles, a repository of everything the Primo had ever researched. Lena believes that vessel is still out there, and I trust her. If anyone can track down the Forge, it's her. That vessel may give us the edge we need."

"We'd better hope it does," Dryker said, grimly. "We don't know how many Void Wraith vessels are out there, but does it matter? They can keep building, harvesting our colonies to make more troops. We need a real solution, and if we approach this like a conventional war we're going to lose."

"Both Nolan and Dryker speak with wisdom, but whether this war is futile or not, it must be fought," Fizgig said. "The Void Wraith will come, and we will drive them back. We need to protect our people, even if we lose our worlds. We must fall back, and give Nolan the time to discover this Forge. Evaluate our respective citizens to humanity's core worlds, then hold there. That defense will take all of us to plan. Humans, Tigris, and Primo."

"Are you willing to appoint Dryker as the supreme commander of the Tigris fleets?" Celendra asked, fixing Fizgig with her unblinking stare.

"I will follow Dryker," Fizgig said, scratching the fur around her arm cast. "I've no doubt he will lead us to victory."

"Then it's settled," Dryker said, looking from person to person. "We'll go over the reports everyone has supplied, and come up with a defensive plan of action. Nolan will hunt down this Forge, and find out how they used it to stop the Void Wraith. It isn't much, but it's what we have."

Exiled

Thank you for reading Void Wraith. If you're enjoying the series, please consider signing up to the mailing list. I'll send you a copy of Exiled, the Destroyer prequel. You'll find out how Nolan ended up on the *Johnston*, and a bit more about the Void Wraith and their motives.

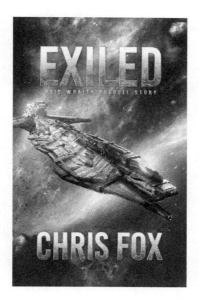

Sign up for the mailing list at chrisfoxwrites.com and read the Destroyer prequel for free.